"Where's Chi...

"She's—" Tory was having trouble breathing.

Taking the younger woman's trembling hands, Phyllis led her to the couch. She responded to Tory's desperation, and her own emotions began to shut down, preparing her for the bad news she sensed was coming.

"Bruce..." Tory tried again.

"He found you," Phyllis said, trying to keep her panic at bay. "He's got Christine." Tory's ex-husband was the reason Christine had accepted the job in Shelter Valley—to get Tory as far away from the man as she could.

Tory shook her head. "He...killed...her..." The last word trailed off into a tormented whisper. "He caught up with us on the New Mexico border."

"What happened?" Phyllis gasped.

"When Christine wouldn't pull over, Bruce started bumping the side of the car, trying to force us to stop." Head down, she played with her fingers. "I don't remember much else. When I came to in the hospital, they told me there'd been a one-car accident—that we'd lost control and driven over a cliff—and that my s-s-sister was dead."

"I'm so sorry..."

Dear Reader,

Welcome back to Shelter Valley! Or, if you're visiting for the first time, all of us who've been here before wish you a warm Shelter Valley welcome. You'll find that just about *everything* here is warm—the welcome, the people, the weather…

On this particular visit to Shelter Valley, you're going to meet Tory Evans. She's only twenty-six but circumstances, experience and a sharp intelligence make her more aware of some things than she'd like to be. You'll get to know Tory from the very beginning of this story—but only you and one other person in Shelter Valley know that she's Tory Evans; everyone else believes she's her older sister, Christine. Tory is lonely, but because she can't tell anyone who she really is, making friends is almost impossible. That's where you come in. I hope you'll be moved by Tory and that she'll find a friend in you—an advocate—to see her through the battle for her freedom.

I think we all fight Tory's battle in one guise or another. Sometimes we're faced with a wrong that seems right—a decision that *looks* right but which, on further reflection, we recognize is wrong. And we're all forced, at some time or other, to confront who we really are, the people life and circumstances have made us— and the possibilities of who we might become.… And ironically, the part that often takes the most courage is being able to see the value that *already* exists within ourselves.

Luckily, Tory is making her search in Shelter Valley, where life's most fundamental truths still form the basis of people's decisions and relationships. In that sense, my home is a mini-Shelter Valley and I find, along with Tory, that knowing what's important, keeping the heart at the heart of the matter, can and does lead to happiness.

So, welcome to Shelter Valley. Travel the road to happiness!

Tara Taylor Quinn

P.S. I love to hear from readers. You can reach me at:
P.O. Box 15065, Scottsdale, AZ 85267-5065 or check out my website at http://members.home.net/ttquinn

My Sister, Myself
Tara Taylor Quinn

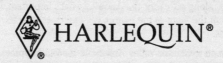

HARLEQUIN®

TORONTO • NEW YORK • LONDON
AMSTERDAM • PARIS • SYDNEY • HAMBURG
STOCKHOLM • ATHENS • TOKYO • MILAN • MADRID
PRAGUE • WARSAW • BUDAPEST • AUCKLAND

ISBN 0-373-70949-8

MY SISTER, MYSELF

Visit us at www.eHarlequin.com

Printed in U.S.A.

For Patty

I pray that you will never run out of answers—
or the willingness to share them with me.

Thank you for opening up my world, and filling my heart.

PROLOGUE

SHE WAS ALMOST there.

Shelter Valley, once a two-day drive away, was now just two miles ahead. How had more than thirty hours passed without her being aware? What had she driven by along the way?

Was she going to take the exit? Or wasn't she?

How could she possibly make a decision when she wasn't ready?

If Christine didn't show up to take this job, she'd lose it.

Another green sign whizzed by the passenger window of Tory's new Ford Mustang. *Shelter Valley, 1 mile.*

Christine. Tears flowed from Tory's eyes, as they'd been doing for most of the trip, trailing almost unnoticed down her face. *Christine.* So beautiful. So worthy.

What do I do? How do I go on without you?

And then, to herself, *How do I not?*

Tory's life had been spared. That made no sense to her. Justice had not been served.

"What do you want me to do?" she cried to an absent Christine when the silence in the car grew too overwhelming. "Bruce thinks he killed *me,* not you." Pulling over to the shoulder of the road, Tory barely got her car into park before the sobs broke loose.

Her beloved older sister had only been dead a week.

Tory was all alone. Completely and totally alone for the first time in her godawful life. And she'd thought, after spending two years fleeing a maniacal ex-husband, that it couldn't get any worse.

Her tearstained face turned toward the sky, she tried, through blurry eyes, to find some guidance from above. Was Christine up there in all that blueness somewhere? Watching over her, guiding her?

There were no answers from up there. But straight ahead was another green sign with fluorescent white lighting. *Shelter Valley, this exit.*

Twenty-six-year-old Tory Evans had been searching for shelter her entire life. But she'd never found it. Was this time going to be any different?

As long as Bruce thought her dead, she'd be safe from him.

Coming from old New England money, he had widespread influence. His tentacles were everywhere. They'd infiltrated every city, every small town, every hut she'd ever inhabited while trying to evade him. Bruce Taylor had never been denied. His mother, having found him perfect in every way, had refused to allow any kind of discipline in his life— still refused to see that her grown son was less than exemplary, making excuses for him at every infraction. And his father, a shipping magnate, had assuaged the guilt of his neglect with everything money could buy. He'd even bought off someone in the legal system the one time Tory had gone to the law for help regarding Bruce's physical abuse. Somehow the tables had been turned on her, the innuendoes so twisted that Tory had known, even before she'd faced the judge, that she was going to lose.

She would never have gotten her divorce if she'd gone about it the normal way—filing, having him served. In her desperation, she'd come up with a pretty clever plan: coaxing Bruce to accompany her on a Tiajuana get-away and then, in the middle of his three-day drunk, taking him to the local courthouse for a quickie divorce. He'd demanded the divorce be nullified. She wouldn't agree to it, but he still hadn't accepted her no.

At thirty, Bruce didn't know the meaning of the word no. He took what he wanted, accepted it as his due. And he wanted Tory. Was obsessed with keeping possession of his ex-wife. The only way to be safe from him was to be dead. To stay dead. And to let Christine live.

It was never going to work.

CHAPTER ONE

BEN SANDERS approached the Shelter Valley exit with trepidation. Maybe he shouldn't have come. There were other places to get a good education. Other places to start over. What if the town was nothing more than a few old buildings, some houses and a street or two? What if it wasn't home?

He'd heard about Shelter Valley his whole life, heard it described as a town where people cared, where they looked out for one another. A place where family mattered. He hoped it was true.

Signaling his turn, Ben guided the Ford F-150 from the highway, slowing as he came to the end of the ramp.

With everything he owned packed in boxes and stacked in the bed of his truck, he took the turn toward Shelter Valley, glancing avidly around him. He had no idea what he was looking for. Something he recognized, maybe. But no matter what his boyhood imaginings told him, he knew there would be nothing. He'd never been here before.

Except in his heart.

He'd been hearing the story of his grandmother's journey from Shelter Valley since before he was old enough to understand its significance—a fourteen-year-old girl separated from her family, from the strong father she'd adored, from the only way of life she'd ever known. That story was the one piece of family lore his father had ever shared with him.

Shelter Valley had been beckoning him ever since. Maybe because of the nomadic way he'd grown up. Or maybe he'd inherited more than his share of his great-grandfather's genes. Maybe old Samuel Montford was calling him to come home.

Maybe he'd just built up some stupid fantasy of a home because at the age of twenty-six he'd never had a real one.

The town came into view in a hurry. Over a hill, and there it was, out in the desert right where his great-grandfather had left it. Surrounded by hard ground and cacti, the town of his dreams had a color scheme of shades of brown and a backdrop of majestic mountains. Slowing the truck as he drove into Shelter Valley, Ben tried to notice everything at once. The neighborhoods, what he could see of them, looked nice, nothing fancy for the most part, but clean and well kept. There were people about, an old woman pruning a rosebush, some kids playing with a ball on the sidewalk, a teenage girl roller-skating alongside him.

He let her pass.

This time was for him. He wanted to savor it alone.

A few mansions sat interspersed on the distant mountain ahead of him. He wondered if a Montford lived in one of those houses. If there were even any Montfords left in this town.

He'd always believed he had family here.

More wishful thinking of a lonely boy.

Ben wasn't a boy anymore. Marriage had cured him of that. Raising and supporting the child he'd believed was his had finished the job. Or maybe it'd been losing her—

No! He'd promised himself he wasn't going to allow himself those thoughts, those memories. The pain. Not ever. He had a new life now. The one that had been interrupted during his senior year in high school. He was going it alone, counting on the only person he knew he could count on—himself. No more looking back.

His new address was on a piece of paper that lay on the seat beside him—an apartment in an older home near the campus of Montford University. Classes started in two days, but it wouldn't take him that long to get ready. He'd already registered by mail and phone, only had a few books left to buy. Some boxes to unpack.

Eight years later than he'd planned, he was starting college.

Slowing even more as he neared downtown Shelter Valley—a strip of stores on both sides of Main Street, with angled parking along the curbs—Ben smiled. The Valley Diner, with its forest-green awning, Weber's department store, the drugstore, were all just as he'd imagined. Almost as if someone had crept into his boyhood fantasies, stolen the images and dropped them here for him to find all these years later.

And then, as he reached the intersection at Main and Montford, he noticed the statue holding pride of place in the town square. Surrounded by lush green and carefully cropped grass, the life-size sculpture sparkled with a newness that reminded him of Christmas. Its polished stone surfaces glistened beneath the setting Arizona sun. The placard was so big he could read it from the road.

With a rush of incomprehensible feeling, Ben pulled his truck into the first empty spot he found, locked it up—kind of pointless considering all the stuff piled in the back—and as though compelled, headed straight for the statue. He read every word of the brief biography typed in smaller print on the placard before allowing himself his first real look.

He'd been waiting all his life for this moment.

And he wasn't disappointed.

Incredulous, his heart full, Ben stared up at the likeness of his great-grandfather. The sculpted features were solid and real, almost as though Samuel Montford would come to life if the sun got warm enough. And as Ben stood and stared at the man who'd lived so many years ago, he could have been looking in a mirror.

A couple strolled by hand in hand, engrossed in each other, but they smiled at Ben as they passed. He smiled back. He wanted to ask if they saw the resemblance, half expected them to notice without his asking. They might have, too, if they'd ever fully looked his way.

There'd be time for that later. The rest of his life.

Bidding his great-grandfather a silent "See ya later," Ben strode eagerly toward his truck. The apartment he'd never seen before was calling him. He'd come home.

"COME ON, CHRISTINE, where are you?" Dr. Phyllis Langford paced in front of her living-room window, watching the road intently. She found herself playing an old childhood game: Christine's would be the fifth car to drive down her street. No, the tenth...

Catching a glimpse of her reflection in the window, she was a little frightened by the tension she read there. Even framed by her flyaway red hair, her face looked stiff, unyielding.

With Christine already weeks later than she should have been, Phyllis was growing more and more anxious to see her, to know that her friend was all right. Daylight passed into darkness, and still Christine didn't arrive. Her note, obviously quickly scrawled, had said today was the day.

It had said nothing about the car accident that had delayed her. Nothing to convey to Phyllis the extent of Christine's injuries, the damage to her car, how Tory had fared. Cryptic to the point of impersonal, the scribbled note had merely said she'd be arriving this afternoon.

Afternoon was over now.

Driven from her quaint little house by an energy

she didn't understand, Phyllis stood out by the curb, watching for headlights. Something was wrong.

Her heart twisted as she thought of her friend, and the tortured life she'd led. Shelter Valley was supposed to be Christine's new beginning. A life where good was possible—and where evil was left far behind. A time for healing. A time for Christine and her younger sister, Tory, to nurture each other.

With a doctorate in psychology, Phyllis fully understood the steps the sisters would have to take, the stages they'd pass through on their way to emotional freedom from their abusive past. But it was as a friend that she intended to be with them, to accompany them on that journey.

Back in her house, Phyllis rechecked the room that Christine and Tory would be sharing. The twin beds were made. The closet full of hangers. The new dressers empty and waiting.

School was due to start on Monday. As the newest psychology professor at Montford University, Phyllis had been ready for the semester to begin weeks ago. Christine, the new English professor, hadn't had the same time to prepare. She had her lessons planned; she'd shipped them—and all her books and research materials—ahead of her. But still, she'd left herself too little time to acclimate to her new home in Arizona—a far cry from the New England city they'd left—and to Montford's campus, the small town, the people here.

Not to mention the new climate, Phyllis thought, going in to change the short-sleeved knit shirt she'd pulled on over knee-length shorts earlier that afternoon. Even with the air conditioner running, she couldn't seem to stop sweating. Arizona's heat might be dry, but Phyllis certainly wasn't.

Maybe when Christine got settled in, she could help Phyllis lose some weight. She'd offered to help back when they'd lived next door to each other in Boston, but at that time Phyllis had still been punishing herself because of a husband who'd preferred another woman's body to her own. Her plumpness had been what she'd deserved.

Then.

Christine and Tory weren't the only ones reinventing themselves. In the weeks since she'd arrived in Shelter Valley, Phyllis had changed, too. Already she'd made some friends. Close friends. Becca and Will Parsons and their darling new daughter, Bethany. Becca's sister, Sari. Martha Moore and John Strickland. Linda Morgan, the associate dean at Montford. Will's energetic youngest sister, Randi. Most of them friends she knew would still be in her life thirty years from now.

Because of their big hearts and their willingness to accept a stranger as one of them, Phyllis had begun to value herself again.

And she knew that if Christine was ever going to find peace on this earth, Shelter Valley was the place.

Having waited so long for the doorbell to ring, Phyllis felt her heart jump alarmingly when it finally did. She flew to the door, flung it open and pulled the young woman standing on the front step into her arms.

"I'm so glad you guys are finally here," she said, tearing up with relief.

"Yeah." Tory was crying, too.

"Where's Christine?" Phyllis asked, urging Tory into the house as she looked past her.

There was a new Mustang in her driveway. An empty Mustang.

Dread crawled over her as she turned slowly back. But there was no reason to think the worst.

"Where's Christine?" she asked again. Back in Boston there'd been reason to worry, but Christine would be fine now.

"She's…" Tory seemed to be having trouble breathing. "He…Bruce…"

Taking the younger woman's trembling hands, Phyllis led her to the couch. Phyllis responded to Tory's desperation, and her own emotions began to shut down, preparing her for the bad news she sensed was coming.

"Bruce…" Tory tried again.

But Phyllis didn't need to hear. Tory's sobs were so filled with anguish Phyllis was choking, too.

"He found you," she said, trying to keep her own panic at bay. "He's got Christine."

Tory's ex-husband was the reason Christine had accepted the job at Montford—to get Tory as far away from the man as she could.

Tory shook her head. "He…killed her…" The last word trailed off into a tormented whisper.

Numb with shock, Phyllis sat with Tory, held her, comforted her, but she had no idea what she was saying. Had a feeling it didn't much matter, that Tory had no idea what she was saying, either. A solitary tear stole down Phyllis's cheek.

Damn.

She'd known something was wrong. She'd *known* it.

"How did it happen?" she asked softly, more because the only part of her mind currently working, the analytical part, knew Tory needed to get everything out.

Christine's life was over. Her struggle was over. Phyllis just couldn't believe it.

"Somehow he discovered that we were heading out here," Tory said, her voice weak from crying. Her slim, perfectly sculpted frame and beautiful face were sagging with strain. Watching her, Phyllis was taken aback at how much she resembled her sister. She'd thought so when she'd first met Tory earlier in the summer.

Not many months ago, Christine had sat on this same couch back in Boston, her body bent in defeat, her big blue eyes—exact replicas of Tory's—dark with shadows as she recounted for Phyllis the horrors of her childhood.

As Phyllis had then, she sat quietly now, allowing the other sister to do her telling in her own time.

"He caught up with us at the New Mexico border."

Oh, God. The landscape was so barren there. Hot. Unyielding.

"He kept motioning for us to pull over, but Christine wouldn't."

Tory's eyes filled with helpless tears again as she looked at Phyllis. "I told her to stop," she said. "He wanted me, not her."

"Unless he was angry with her for taking you away from him," Phyllis offered, already seeing the blame and guilt Tory was heaping on herself.

Tory shook her head, her short blond hair bouncing with the vigorous movement. "He only ever wanted me," she said, her voice bitter. "Other people don't matter enough to make him angry." She paused, her eyes dead-looking. "In his mind, there's no one alive who can beat him. People are merely ants he occasionally has to step on."

Though she'd heard such things before—in clinical settings—Phyllis was sickened by the description. And by young Tory's far-too-mature account of the man who'd made her life a living hell.

"So what happened when Christine finally stopped?" Phyllis coaxed softly when it appeared she'd lost Tory to places Phyllis had never been— places she probably couldn't even imagine.

Tory shook her head, hands trembling. "She didn't stop," Tory whispered, her eyes wide with horror.

"She told me I was the only good thing in her life, the only thing worth living for, and she wouldn't stop."

"You sound like that surprises you," Phyllis said.

"If it hadn't been for me, Christine's life would have been perfect once she left home," she said sincerely. "I let her down so many times. I didn't go to college. I married Bruce. I ran from everything."

Remembering that she knew things Tory didn't, Phyllis chose her words carefully. "Christine chose Bruce for you, Tory," she said, revealing the part she could.

"What?" the young woman asked, shocked. "How? She couldn't have. I met him at a party."

"And when you brought him home, when she met him, knew that he came from a good family, a wealthy family, she did everything she could to throw the two of you together." Phyllis repeated what Christine herself had confessed all those months ago. "She thought he was your ticket out."

Silently Tory listened, her gaze turned inward, as though she was remembering back to the unreal days of her courtship.

"She did, didn't she?" Phyllis finally asked.

"I don't know," Tory said, her brow furrowed. "I guess. Yeah, she was kind of always there, encouraging me, helping me get ready for dates, choosing just the right clothes for me to wear. But then, she was my older sister. She was supposed to do that."

Feeling the other woman's confusion, her pain, Phyllis smoothed the bangs from Tory's eyes—and saw, for the first time, the ugly red scar marring Tory's forehead just beneath her hairline.

"What happened?" she gasped.

Tory rearranged her bangs self-consciously. "When Christine wouldn't pull over, Bruce got more and more reckless, bumping into the side of the car, trying to force us to stop." Head down, she played with her fingers. "I don't remember much else," she confessed. Tears dropped onto her hand. "When I came to in the hospital, they told me there'd been a one-car accident—no one's fault. We'd lost control on a curve and driven over a cliff—and that my s-s-sister was dead."

Phyllis drew the young woman into her arms. "Oh, Tory, honey, I'm so sorry," she whispered, over and over again, as her own tears fell on Tory's hair.

Oh, Christine. Dear, sweet, tortured Christine. Have you finally found your peace?

TORY COULDN'T BELIEVE she'd slept. Coming slowly awake Saturday morning in the comfortable bed, the comfortable room, feeling almost rested, she wondered at first if she was still dreaming. A dream she didn't ever want to wake from.

She glanced sleepily around the room and saw the luggage she and Phyllis had carried in the night before, the new dresser—and the empty twin bed across from her own.

For Christine.

That split second was all it took for everything to come tumbling back. The dread. The fear. The soul-crushing despair.

"You awake?" Phyllis's voice followed a brief knock on the door.

"Yeah, come in." Tory quickly pulled her bangs down over her forehead. After years of hiding bruises, the action was purely instinctive.

"Good morning." Phyllis smiled, carrying a cup of coffee, which she set on Tory's bedside table.

Being waited on in bed warmed Tory even more than the coffee Phyllis had brought.

They discussed trivial things for a while—the unbelievably hot Arizona weather, the pretty house Phyllis had found in August when she'd preceded Christine out to Shelter Valley. Also some of the people she'd met. People Tory would likely meet.

Trying to listen, to absorb, Tory settled for concentrating on Phyllis's smile, instead, the steady cadence of her voice, the calm strength she emanated as she sat in the middle of Christine's bed. Her nerves bouncing on the edge of her skin, Tory somehow made herself stay put, made her thoughts stay put. Forced down the panic inside her.

Phyllis was being so darn nice. Other than Christine, no one had ever been so nice to her before. And for no reason that she could fathom.

"We're going to have to call Dr. Parsons and let him know Christine isn't coming," Phyllis finally said gently.

Here it comes, Tory thought, taking a deep breath.

She'd rehearsed the speech. A hundred times on her trek across the barren New Mexico and northern Arizona landscape.

Another deep breath, and still nothing happened. She couldn't do it.

"Life insurance was part of her benefits package," Phyllis said, her eyes full of compassion. "I know Christine's was already in effect because it was done at the same time as mine. We can give Dr. Parsons a copy of her death certificate, and at least you won't have any financial worries."

Tory stared at her.

"I'm counting on you to stay right here with me, just like we planned," Phyllis continued. "Until you have time to decide what you want to do, anyway. It's kind of lonely having an entire house to myself after living in an apartment for so long," she said, obviously giving Tory whatever time she needed to enter the conversation. "I guess I need to hear life on the other side of my walls."

"There isn't one," Tory stated bluntly.

Phyllis frowned. "Isn't one what?"

"Death certificate."

"But—"

"At least, not for Christine."

"I don't understand." Phyllis was still frowning. "The hospital told you your sister was dead, but no one signed a death certificate?" Her face cleared. "If they haven't seen her body, she may still be alive." She looked at Tory. "Maybe Bruce has her, after all."

Watching the expressions chase themselves across Phyllis's face, Tory shook her head.

"The hospital authorities saw her." She paused,

swallowed. "I...saw...her." Arms wrapped around her drawn-up knees, Tory stared down at the bed. "I had her cremated like she always said she wanted."

Maybe most sisters didn't talk to each other about their burials while still so young, but she and Christine had. With the lives they'd lived, the home they'd grown up in, death had been a constant possibility.

"You can't do that without a death certificate."

"I had one," Tory admitted, biting her lip. "Just not Christine's." Her head hurt and her face was numb as she silently spun in the unending loop of terror inside her mind.

"Christine and I look so much alike...."

Chin resting on her knees, Tory studied the bed through blurry eyes. Tears dripped off her face, rolling slowly down the sides of her knees, but her voice was almost steady as she related what she'd been told so compassionately by the clergywoman who'd visited her in the hospital.

Tory's bed sank on one side with Phyllis's weight. She tried to concentrate on the comfort of the other woman's hands rubbing slowly back and forth along her back.

"My driver's license was brand-new. Christine's was six years old...."

The hand on her back slowed, stopped moving, hung there suspended.

"We were both pretty messed up in the crash...."

"Tory—"

"She'd gotten cold, my monogrammed sweater was the only thing within reach for her to put on without stopping and—"

"Oh, my God."

"When word got out that the woman who died in the crash was presumed to be Tory Evans, Bruce, who was apparently beside himself, sent one of the family staff to identify me. Her."

"And the guy did?"

Tory nodded, turned to meet Phyllis's incredulous eyes. "Christine went through the windshield," Tory said, trying not to remember the one brief glimpse she'd had of her sister in the morgue. "Her face was barely recognizable, even to me. She'd just had her hair cut short like mine, said she was embarking on a new life and wanted a new look."

Tory's sigh was ragged. "Apparently when I first came to and they asked me if I knew who I was, I said Christine." She looked at Phyllis again. "I can't remember that at all, but knowing me, knowing how I get when I'm hurting, I would've been calling for Christine...."

Her sister had been her balm her entire life, as far back as Tory could remember. Which was pretty damn far. She'd been only three the first time her stepfather had thrown her against a wall. She could still remember the stars she'd seen. The confusion that had kept her immobile long enough for him to do it again.

"This is incredible," Phyllis said. She took hold of Tory's shoulders, turning Tory to face her.

"They think you're dead, that you've been cremated."

Tory nodded wearily, her eyes overflowing with tears. "The death certificate I have is my own."

CHAPTER TWO

BEN LASTED until midway through Saturday morning. His ground-floor apartment was clean and quiet and comfortably furnished, but now he was at loose ends, and it was only ten o'clock. That was how long it had taken him to get his few pots and pans and dishes and glasses moved in and put away in the appropriate cupboards. And get his computer set up. He'd have done better if he hadn't already put his clothes away and hooked up his stereo the night before.

He'd called Alex last night, too, thankful that she'd answered on his first try. The week before, he'd had to claim a wrong number three times before his daughter had been the one to answer his call. His daughter—not his daughter but the little girl he'd raised and loved as his own. Now that he had a number of his own, the subterfuge wouldn't be necessary. He'd had Alex write down the number, complete with step-by-step instructions on how to call collect, and then made her repeat everything back to him several times. He'd given her his address, too, but didn't expect her to be able to use it. At seven, Alex was bright enough to write him a letter and address the envelope, but she'd have to go to her mother for a stamp, and Mary would certainly deny the request. Ben wasn't Alex's real father—her birth father—though Mary had neglected to tell him so until recently. Now she wanted Ben out of their lives. Out of Alex's life.

Damn her for putting Alex and him in this situation. Besides, the courts had said he and Alex should remain in contact, despite the fact that he was divorced from her mother and had no biological claim on her.

He headed out and spent an hour and a half at the local grocery store, stocking up not only on food but on every single household item he thought he might need at some point in his life.

Cleansers, a mop and bucket, sponges, a couple kinds of dishwashing cloths, several kitchen-towel sets, shoe inserts, extra laces and polish, bandages and antiseptic. Aspirin, cold tablets, cough syrup, paper towels. Toilet paper, tissues and a sewing kit, too.

Anything and everything that seemed to belong in a home, he bought.

The girl at the checkout made eyes at him as he went through.

"You new in town?" she asked with an appreciative smile.

"I am." Ben glanced around for the name of the store, scribbling it on a check.

"Looks like you're planning to be here a while."

"Yes." He signed the bottom of the check and waited for the total.

After a few more failed attempts to snare his attention, she finished ringing him up.

He was glad to collect his bags and be gone. The girl had been cute. Friendly. Twenty or twenty-one. If he'd met her in another life, he might even have smiled back at her.

But not in *this* life. At least not until he had his college degree and a career that satisfied him. He'd wasted eight years already. There were no more to waste.

After a brief detour to visit his great-grandfather, Ben was home again, slowly and methodically unloading his purchases. The first-aid stuff had to go in the bathroom medicine cabinet. Everyone knew that. And the kitchen towels in a drawer by the sink. One he draped over the oven door handle. He'd seen that on television once.

Down to just the sewing kit, he wasn't sure where to put it. He finally settled on a drawer in the bathroom. Chances were, if he ever needed it, it would be when he was getting dressed and pulled off a button. Wouldn't be much call for it otherwise. Sewing on buttons was about the only thing Ben could do with a needle and thread.

Not even noon yet, and he had a day and a half to kill before school started. Ben rearranged some things in the kitchen—and then moved them back to their original places, deciding he'd made the best choice the first time around.

George Winston's *Autumn* piano music drifted through the apartment, but as he made one more trek from room to room to make sure there wasn't anything more he could do, Ben felt the quiet—the absence of life—a weight pressing down on him.

He was used to noise—childish laughter and shrieks, blocks tumbling, play dishes being washed. And a woman's whines trailing behind him with every step he took.

Ben got his keys again, and went back out to his truck. He had a home now. His own home. One where he'd be spending the next few years. Where he could call the shots.

It was time to get a dog.

"WHY DIDN'T YOU TELL the authorities they'd made a mistake? That Christine was the one who died in the accident?" Phyllis asked Tory later that morning.

She'd had a phone call earlier, and then Tory had asked if she could shower off the grime of the drive. She'd been too exhausted, mentally and physically, to do so the night before. When she'd come out of the shower, Phyllis had placed Tory's suitcases on her bed and was standing by with an empty hanger, ready to help her unpack.

Now they were sitting at Phyllis's kitchen table, the remains of a late breakfast neither of them had really wanted, or eaten much of, in front of them.

Why *hadn't* she told the authorities? Tory had known the question was coming.

"I started to," she said, sweating in spite of the air-conditioned kitchen. She was wearing jeans and a T-shirt, regardless of Phyllis's warning about the Arizona heat, but it wasn't the clothes that were making her uncomfortable. It was the task ahead of her.

She was about to find out just how insane she was. And what little chance her half-born hope of freedom really had.

"I fully intended to tell them, but when I opened my mouth, nothing came out. At first, everyone just figured I was too distraught to speak. Whenever I tried to tell them the truth, they'd tell me to get some rest, or they'd pat my arm and say they understood."

Phyllis's hand covered Tory's. Tory gently pulled her hand away.

"Then it hit me," Tory said, her gaze pleading as it met Phyllis's. "As soon as I told them and word got out, Bruce would be right back on my tail. I only wanted a couple of days to rest, to think, to plan. So I let them think I *was* Christine. But as one day turned into the next, I couldn't make myself become Tory again and...and take on all that fear."

"I don't know how you lived with it as long as you did."

Tory smiled bitterly. "What other choice did I have?"

Phyllis moved the salt and pepper shakers. "So what are you thinking now?"

"That as long as I'm Christine, I'm safe."

"Christine has a job to do starting Monday."

"I know," Tory said, her throat dry.

"Christine said you never finished college."

"I never even *went* to college. Bruce didn't want me on campus with all the college boys."

Both women were silent, the words they weren't speaking hanging in the air. How could Tory possibly be Christine? Christine was a college professor.

"You could always quit the job."

"And go where? Do what? My résumé says I'm a professor."

Every possibility had already occurred to Tory. She knew there was no way this could work. No way she could convince herself this was even a little bit right. She was just too weak to face the alternative.

"Bruce will probably keep tabs on Christine for a little while. If she's alive, she has to be teaching college. Anything else will make him suspicious."

"The bastard should be in prison."

Tory couldn't travel that road. If she did, her bitterness would destroy her.

"I have two choices," she said, pushing congealed eggs around on her plate. "Either I come clean and spend the rest of my life trying to hide from Bruce and wearing his bruises every time I fail, or I show up at Montford University on Monday morning and teach English."

She used to believe there was a difference between right and wrong. That for every situation there was a correct choice, the *right* choice. She'd even vowed, when her married life had first become a living hell, worse than the life she'd had growing up, to always make that right choice. She'd believed it would eventually deliver her from cruelty, from pain.

She didn't believe that anymore.

"The boxes Christine shipped are in the closet in the spare bedroom," Phyllis said. "I'm using it as an office."

Tory watched the other woman scrape their uneaten food into the garbage, and then stack the two plates.

"Her lessons plans are in there," Phyllis continued, speaking unemotionally, as though they were discussing nothing more serious than what movie they were going to see. "They'll be clear, concise and very detailed. You've got thirty-six hours before school starts."

Heart pounding, Tory said, "You don't think I should even consider trying this, do you."

Phyllis looked Tory straight in the eye, her expression grave. "I don't see that you have any other choice."

Tory held Phyllis's gaze for as long as she could stand it, then dropped her eyes.

"What would Christine think?" she whispered, the guilt rising up to choke her. *She* should be dead, not Christine. She'd have gladly given her life if it meant saving Christine's.

"She's watching over you, Tory. Can't you feel

her?'' Phyllis lowered her voice to a rough whisper, but the sharp conviction behind her words was unmistakable.

Tears in her eyes, Tory shook her head. She wanted so badly to believe that Christine was still with her. She could hardly even breathe when she thought about facing the rest of her life without her sister. But she couldn't be sure of anything anymore. Did Christine really want her to do this? Or was Tory's mind, influenced by her cowardice, playing some sick game with her?

''Christine told me once, not too long ago, that you were her only reason for living,'' Phyllis said. ''You were the only good thing in or about her life.''

''She told me that, too, but she was just being kind. It didn't really mean anything. How could it? She was an incredible woman, had the whole world at her feet.''

''She didn't think so.''

The sincerity in Phyllis's voice grabbed Tory, holding her until she had to admit that Phyllis might know more about her sister's mental state in the past few years than she did herself.

''She would insist that you do this, Tory,'' Phyllis said firmly. ''And she'd want me to help you in any way I can.''

''WILL—DR. PARSONS—only met Christine once. Months ago. She's had her hair cut since then. Lost some weight...''

The two women were in the bedroom Phyllis had turned into an office, sitting on the floor and surrounded by opened packing boxes. They'd been at it most of the day, Phyllis administering the fastest teacher-education course in history.

"Our eyes are what people notice most about us," Tory said, trying, for Phyllis's sake if nothing else, to get into the spirit of the plan.

"They're beautiful," Phyllis said gently. "So large and such a striking blue. But mostly so expressive."

Tory leafed through the pages of the American literature anthology she held on her lap.

"They were one of the first things I noticed about Christine," Phyllis added.

The familiar pang clutched Tory's insides. "I'm so sorry, Phyllis," she said, dropping a lesson plan for the third week of classes as she looked up. "I've been weeping all over the place about losing my sister, but you also lost a great deal, didn't you? The way Christine talked about you, the two of you must have been very close."

Tears brimmed in Phyllis's eyes, but her ready smile was evident, too. "We were. Your sister was very special."

Tory nodded, a measure of peace loosening the knots in her stomach. "I think you must be very special, too," she said softly. "Do you know you're the first real friend Christine ever had?"

"No," Phyllis said, her eyes wide. "I know she was a private person, but as sweet as she was, I'm sure there were others who scaled those walls of hers.''

Scaled those walls. The words were threatening to Tory. She and Christine both had their walls. And the security in that was to think them unscalable.

"Our colleagues at the college all flocked to her," Phyllis said. She was assembling materials for the fourth week's lesson plan. "It must have been the same for her in college. You probably just never met any of her friends, since she was five years older than you."

"She never had a friend," Tory said with complete certainty.

Any chance of friendship had ended when they'd tried to report their stepfather's abuse. Everyone had been shocked. Ronald was well-known in the community, soft-spoken, active at church. He'd car-pooled. He'd protested his innocence, incredibly hurt by then-twelve-year-old Christine's allegations. They'd been assigned a caseworker, but of course there'd been nothing to find. Ronald had simply not had anything alcoholic to drink during the weeks of the investigation.

And the confusing cruel truth was, when Ronald wasn't drinking, he hadn't been a bad father to them.

They'd been made to feel so ashamed of their complaints they'd begun to blame themselves for the abuse. They'd also lost all faith in the system that was purported to protect them.

"She lived at home when she went to college— probably because our stepfather wasn't as rough with me when he had two of us to torment," Tory said slowly. "Never once did she go out. Not on a date. Not to study. Nor did she ever have anyone over."

Neither of them had. Neither had had the courage to risk bringing another person into their home. For that person's sake. And for their own.

Bearing the violence privately was bad enough; to have it made known to others would have been intolerable. At least with no one else knowing, when they left the house, they left the violence behind. While they were safely at school, they were free. The real world was an escape neither of them had been willing to jeopardize.

"OKAY, THE FIRST THING to remember when you walk into the classroom is that you're the boss."

Exhausted, yet filled with nervous excitement, Tory sat on her bed, taking notes as Phyllis continued her crash course well past midnight Saturday night. They'd changed into their pajamas hours earlier, but hadn't gotten around to turning in.

"You have to establish your authority immediately, and then you're home free. The most important tool you'll take into that class with you is confidence."

"Kinda hard to be confident when they're all going to know more about my subject than I do," Tory said dryly.

"We'll take care of that," Phyllis replied, her entire body exuding positive energy. "Luckily you're teaching five sections of American lit this semester. You'll be teaching the same material five times, in other words. Now, we have all day tomorrow, to study the textbooks and Christine's notes. For this next week, you only need to know Emerson and Thoreau, and you're already familiar with a lot of that.'' She was sitting on Christine's bed, her legs crossed, her red hair framing her pretty face as though she'd just styled it an hour before, instead of the almost eighteen hours it had been.

''Christine said you were extremely intelligent. She said that when she was in college you used to help her study for exams, reading her texts and asking her questions from study guides. According to her, you'd often know the answers as well as she did.''

''Sometimes.''

''You must have a wonderful memory and a very acute, analytical brain.'' Phyllis smiled. ''Christine mentioned that you had some pretty stirring debates and some real differences of opinion. You're obviously a natural.''

''Hardly,'' Tory said, but she warmed at the compliment.

Phyllis twisted the opal ring she wore on her right ring finger. ''Have you ever had your IQ tested?''

''No!'' And Tory had no intention of doing so. ''I'd hate to find out that I'm not as smart as I think I am.''

''What if you found out you were smarter?''

Tory was silent for a moment, wondering if her

numbed mind was going to take in everything it had to in the next twenty-four hours. "I think I'd hate that, too," she admitted softly. "Because then I'd know just how much I've wasted, how much I've lost."

"Hey," Phyllis said, unfolding her legs as she reached across to squeeze Tory's hand. "It's not too late. You've got a whole new life ahead of you. Amazing things to accomplish."

Tory smiled, but inside, the familiar dread was spreading. Yeah, she had a whole new life.

It just wasn't *her* life.

BEN WAS IN THE KITCHEN of his two-bedroom apartment, paper towel in hand, when his alarm went off Monday morning.

"Okay, little buddy, you and I need to get some things straight," he said, leaving the puddle in the kitchen as he scooped up the puppy and strode back to the master bedroom to turn off the alarm.

"I'm the boss in this house and what I say goes, got that?" He kept the puppy firmly under his arm, out of harm's way, off the carpet, and with those big imploring brown eyes out of his line of vision. Ben had been implored so much in the past two days—and had given in so often—he was making himself sick.

"When I say it's time for bed, bedtime it is." He continued the lecture as he headed back to the mess awaiting him in the kitchen. "That means I lie down, you lie down, and we both sleep. There will be no barking.'' He stepped over the gate he'd put up across the kitchen doorway. ''No whining. And *if*—that's a big if—I deign to take you into the bedroom with me, there will be no more biting on the ears.''

Dropping the wad of paper towels on the puddle beneath the kitchen table, Ben soaked up the deposit, threw the towels in the special trash bag that would leave the house with him that morning, poured a generous amount of disinfectant on the soiled spot and with another wad of paper towels mopped that up, too.

Only then did he put the puppy down. One set of urine-wet paw prints traipsing across the floor was enough for him. He was learning quickly.

Buddy, which was what Ben had called the dog so far, darted around puppy-style, falling as much as he ran, coming to rest suddenly by a leg of the kitchen table.

''No!'' Ben hollered, grabbing him up before more damage was done. He took the puppy out the sliding glass door off the kitchen and out into the yard, where the little guy did his business. Ben was pleased. Between the two of them, they'd gotten it right that time.

Yes, Ben praised himself, all in all, the training was coming along nicely.

Shut in the bathroom with Ben, Buddy whined the entire time Ben was in the shower. Whether because he missed his master or because the sound of water scared him, Ben wasn't sure.

And because it couldn't be proved either way, he chose to believe that Buddy missed him.

"I've got school this morning, Bud," he said as he dried off, pulled on some briefs and stood before the mirror to shave.

Buddy chewed on his toes.

And then on the new bath rug Ben had purchased the day before to replace the one Buddy had chewed Saturday night when Ben had shut the puppy in the bathroom so he could get some sleep.

"We've already been over this," Ben explained as he pulled the rug off the floor and flung it over the side of the tub. "No chewing on my things. Not on me, my rugs, my clothes or shoes, not anything that I don't hand directly to you. Got that?"

The eight-week-old wad of fur stared up at him, his big brown eyes expectant as he waited for the games to begin anew.

"Don't forget, my man, Zack said I could bring you back if I found you were too much to handle," Ben threatened.

Zack Foster was the local vet—half of the Shelter Valley veterinarian clinic's team. Zack's partner, Cassie, had been out of the office—out of town—when Ben went there Saturday, looking to start his new family. He and Zack had hit it off immediately, spending half an hour talking about the town, what there was to do in the area, baseball scores and the chances of the Phoenix Suns making it to the play-offs that year. By the time he'd gotten around to his reason for being there, Ben had gladly taken the runt-of-the-litter Zack couldn't find a home for. He'd given away the other three, but he'd had no takers for this one—and now Ben thought he knew why. But he'd assured Zack that no six-pound squat-bellied thing whose front and back legs couldn't agree was going to get the better of him.

There was no way, after that grandiose speech, that Ben could return the little bugger. But Buddy didn't have to know that. It wasn't beneath Ben to use whatever tactics he must to establish his authority in the house, once and for all.

Ready for class, in spite of his high-maintenance housemate, Ben was just about to head out when he made a mistake. He looked at those big brown eyes.

Dropping his backpack on the floor, Ben ran to his bedroom, grabbed the only spare blanket from the linen closet, ran back to the kitchen and made a bed for the little guy against a cupboard—on top of which stood the radio, turned down low and set to a classical station. Moving the water dish, and the potty pad, too, he gave the puppy one last scratch behind the ears.

"Wish me luck."

Slinging his backpack over one shoulder, he locked up and climbed into his truck.

He'd been waiting more than half his life for this day.

It had finally begun.

CHAPTER THREE

THE CAMPUS WAS beautiful. Though grass was at a premium in this desert town, Montford's lawns were green and lush, so velvety thick Tory had an urge to lie down in it and pass the day there.

She might have, too, if her kill-'em-with-love drill sergeant wasn't marching along beside her. Students milled all around them, moving with purpose, every single one of them looking as though they belonged.

"You're going to do fine," Phyllis was saying. Not that Tory had expressed her fears this morning. Phyllis just knew she was feeling them.

"You're sure you tested me on every aspect of the Emerson years?" Tory asked for the third time that morning.

"You know it, Tory," Phyllis assured her. "You had a lot of it down before we even started yesterday."

Tory shrugged, feeling stiff in her sister's suit and low heels. Tory was used to less-formal clothes. And higher heels. Christine's feet had been half a size larger than Tory's, but Phyllis had fixed that with some inserts. They'd go shopping for Tory's school clothes later in the week.

"I had no idea I'd retained so much from when I helped Christine study."

"I'd guess it was a good diversion from whatever else might have been going on in your house."

Tory stumbled, still not used to Phyllis's open way of talking about her and Christine's painful upbringing. She wondered how Christine had dealt with her friend's honesty. Wished, suddenly engulfed by an unexpected surge of grief, that Christine were there so she could ask her.

"You've had your meeting with Dr. Parsons," Phyllis said, motioning toward the sidewalk on the left when they came to a fork. "He didn't suspect anything, and he was your toughest sell. The others who interviewed Christine only saw her for a few minutes back in April and then never spoke with her again. Christine got her hair cut. Had a makeover and lost a little weight over the summer, most recently due to her car accident."

"Dr. Parsons sure was nice," Tory said, relaxing just a little as she replayed her early-morning meeting with the president of Montford University. He'd asked about the car accident and been very sympathetic about her sister's death, agreeing not to say anything to anyone else about it, as no one knew her sister or knew that her sister had been coming to town. He understood her need to grieve in private. "He seemed to have a real affection for Christine, though he seemed surprised that she cut her hair."

"*You* cut your hair," Phyllis corrected, slowing as they came to the side door of an old brick building. "You can't keep thinking of Christine as someone else if you're going to pull this off."

Tory looked up at the imposing building, afraid that it was their destination, that Christine's new office, her new colleagues, were in there.

"You make it sound as though we're criminals," Tory told Phyllis, staving off the panic that could send her right back into Bruce's clutches.

"I'm not up on criminal law," Phyllis said, "but I wouldn't be surprised to learn that we're breaking a couple of laws."

Tory had been so caught up with the emotional trauma inherent in the entire situation, she hadn't even given a thought to the legal issues.

"You know, I've spent years ignoring the laws that were supposed to help me, because in my case they never worked. So I've never even thought about the ones I might be breaking."

She looked at her new friend, an angel sent to her from heaven—if there was a heaven. And turned to leave.

"Where are you going?"

"We can't do this, Phyllis. Risking my life, my freedom, because the alternative is no better, is one thing. But I won't risk yours."

Grabbing Tory's arm, Phyllis pulled her toward the door. "If I am breaking a law, that's my choice," she said firmly. "You may think I'm the only friend Christine had, but I *know* she was the only real friend I've ever had, and I'm not letting her down. Or you, either. Let's go."

Perhaps it was a sign of her cowardice. Or weakness. But Tory went.

And two hours later, when she stepped into the first college classroom she'd ever been in—the first of five she'd be stepping into that week—when she saw the rows of desks, the students sitting there, and walked right past them to the front of the room, she refused to let the weakness show.

She was Christine Evans. The best damn teacher any one of those intimidating intelligent students had ever had.

IN A CHAIR right in the middle of the room—not so far back that he wasn't a part of things and not so close to the front that he missed what was going on behind him—Ben watched as his fellow classmates filed in and took their seats. So far, he was the oldest of the bunch. Not too many seniors took American Literature 101.

Still, he wasn't daunted. Or even the slightest bit disappointed. This was his classroom. His school. His day.

Pulling out the black spiral-bound notebook he'd bought for this class and a new pen, he sat back and waited for his teacher to arrive. C. Evans.

Was "C." a man or a woman?

Listening as a rather immature boy, clearly fresh out of high school, tried to pick up the blond cheerleader-type in the back of the room, Ben smiled. He felt the way Buddy had looked in the bathroom that morning.

Let the games begin.

A young woman walked in just then, clearly fresh out of *her* high school, if the confident tilt of her head was anything to judge by. Ben's euphoria faded just a little as he watched her. Overdressed compared to the rest of the shorts-clad students, she stood out in her proper blue suit and white blouse. And she was far too striking to be wearing the no-nonsense pumps she had on.

What bothered him, though, wasn't her clothes. Or even her confidence. It was the way his nerves tensed when she passed his desk. He'd been looking at female students all morning, and he could have been looking at a herd of cattle for all the reaction they aroused in him.

Staring down at the desktop in front of him, at his notebook lying there ready and open, Ben avoided noticing where the young woman sat. He wasn't in the market for an attraction, a flirtation or a romance. Or anything at all that had to do with a woman. Maybe once he'd graduated, enough time would have elapsed and he'd be willing to venture down that road again. Maybe. But for sure, it would be no sooner than that. He wasn't going back to working till he dropped, working at dead-end jobs just to pay the rent.

"Okay, everybody, let's get started, shall we?"

His gaze shooting toward the front of the room, Ben came to attention. He'd been so set on ignoring one of his fellow students, he hadn't even realized the teacher had come in.

Yes, he had. He just hadn't known she was his teacher.

C. Evans. A woman. The suit.

Damn.

She looked straight at him, almost as though she'd read his thoughts, and Ben received his second jolt of the day. Her eyes, so compelling, so *full,* held his, and he sensed, somehow, that she was speaking to him. And what she had to say was far more intense than anything to do with American literature. For a few brief seconds, it was as though only the two of them were in that room.

"I'm Christine Evans," she said, breaking eye contact with him. After glancing around at the rest of her students, she focused on him again.

Her look wasn't sexual. Wasn't the least bit suggestive. It seemed more as if she was searching for a friend. And that she'd chosen him.

Ben couldn't accept the honor.

Glancing away from her, he observed the rest of the students in the room. Had any of them noticed the odd communication? Had any of them experienced it, as well, when Ms. Evans had looked at them? All the students in his line of vision seemed young, inexperienced, oblivious. So much so they didn't recognize the undercurrents? Or were there simply none being sent their way?

"This syllabus covers the entire semester, and we'll be following it exactly," Ms. Evans was saying, passing around handouts.

She hesitated beside his desk, then dropped the stapled sheets on his notebook and moved on.

"Since I'm brand-new to town, I don't know a single one of you, but I'm usually pretty good with names, and I expect to have them all learned within a couple of days. Until then, please bear with me."

Like him, she was a newcomer.

"We'll take a few minutes to go over the syllabus," she went on, "plus my requirements of you and the expectations for this class, including the weekly essays you'll have to write. Then we'll be moving on to this week's topic, the Emerson years..."

She might be new to town, but she clearly wasn't new to teaching.

Ben settled in, making himself concentrate on what the teacher was saying with the same sheer strength of will that had seen him through eight years of toiling at jobs he hated so he could feed his baby girl. Nothing was going to keep him from getting his college degree.

Nothing.

"BEN? COULD I SEE YOU a minute?"

Ben stopped on the way out of his American literature class on Monday, the second week of class. His teacher wanted to see him.

"Sure." Backpack hanging off one shoulder, he approached her desk. Stupid to feel underdressed in his shorts, T-shirt and sandals, but he did. Didn't seem to matter to Christine Evans that it was over a hundred degrees outside. She'd worn a suit to class all four times they'd met.

Not that Ben had permitted himself to dwell on what the woman wore. At least not when he could help it.

She waited for the other students to finish packing up and leave the room, gathering her own stuff together at the same time. Ben started to sweat. He'd spent far too much of the weekend thinking about his English professor.

What secrets were hiding behind those big blue eyes? What made her expression so shadowed sometimes?

How old was she, anyway? And had she ever been married? Would she think him a fool for the mess he'd made of his own life?

Despite his resolve to allow no feelings to complicate his life, he could feel the woman's sorrow. Maybe because it mirrored his own?

"I just wanted to speak with you about your piece on Thoreau," Christine said when the last student had left the room. "Your portrayal of him as an intensely deep and lonely man, rather than the quack many considered him, was quite moving."

"Thank you."

She asked him a couple of questions about his research and he answered her. When she held the paper out to him, her hand was shaking.

"There's a quarterly newsletter, *The Edifice,* for students of English to publish their work. I'd like to see you submit this to the editor for publication."

Ben met her eyes. And looked away. "You think it's good enough?"

"I do." She nodded. "I've got the submission requirements and the address in my office, if you'd like to come with me now."

No. He had another class to get to, all the way across campus. A finance class. Part of his business major. Although it didn't start for another hour... The main thing was, he couldn't afford to see any more of Christine Evans than the three hours a week he was required to sit in her class.

"That'd be great, if you're sure it's not too much trouble," he heard himself say.

His orders didn't seem to have any more effect on him than they did on Buddy.

SHE WAS A FOOL. Not that this was news to Tory. What in hell was she doing inviting Ben Sanders to her office? In the first place, she didn't belong there. The office really wasn't hers. She'd barely moved in.

In the second, teachers shouldn't have favorites. Especially not students who had a look of knowing about them, a maturity. Students who were so capable. So *reliable*.

"It's obvious you do all your reading," she said as she walked with him across campus. The heat was almost tangible, caressing her skin, and she reveled in its gentleness. Phyllis was having a hard time acclimatizing to Arizona's weather. Tory loved it.

"I thought we were supposed to," he said, shortening his stride to stay beside her. She moved over just slightly, automatically, leaving space between them.

She was still wearing Christine's ill-fitting shoes, too busy studying every night to get into Phoenix for that shopping spree.

"You are!" She grinned, forgetting for a moment that she wasn't a teacher walking with a student. "But I'd guess some of my students haven't even bought the text."

"Then they're idiots, wasting this opportunity."

Tory wondered if he meant that.

"Do you like the Emerson years, Ben?" He'd certainly challenged her thinking a time or two during class with his insightful interpretations. She'd rather enjoyed debating with him. In the safety of the classroom.

"Not particularly."

"Oh!" With heat flooding her face, Tory felt once again like the untutored young woman she was. "Well—"

"Don't get me wrong," he interrupted, moving far enough ahead to turn and walk backward, facing her. "It's not that I don't think your class is great. I do. I'm just not particularly fond of the Emerson era." He shrugged. "Too stuffy for me."

"So what authors *are* you fond of?" Passing a couple of girls from one of her other classes, she waved to them, feeling almost like one of them, accompanied as she was by the man they were all drooling over.

Except that she wasn't drooling. Tory had given up drooling. She could relax a bit, though, as long as Ben was in front of her like that.

He shrugged again, fell back into step beside her. "Nathaniel Hawthorne. James Fenimore Cooper."

"You go for the witches and wars, huh?" She moved sideways, leaving a little more space between them.

"What I admire most about *The Last of the Mohicans* is not the battles."

"What is it?"

"Hawkeye."

"Of course. The hero who conquers all and gets his woman." Tory had a problem with that story. She'd wanted to believe there really were heroic men like Cooper's Hawkeye, had held steadfast to that hope even in high school, despite the damage her stepfather had done. She'd held it until she'd met Bruce, married him and found out that no matter what their station, all men were alike.

"No. Hawkeye's a man who has such a sense of honor and decency that he'll risk everything he has, everything he *is*, to see justice done."

Tory stopped in her tracks, her heart beating heavily in her chest. And then started walking again.

There was no point in arguing with him, in telling him that it was just such viewpoints, beliefs, that hurt people like her so badly. People who still believed that the sort of people they read about in books actually existed. There was no point in getting into it with him because she couldn't support her argument with the facts.

"So who's your favorite nineteenth-century American author?" he asked as they neared her office building.

"Louisa May Alcott."

"Hmm. Kind of a minor player, isn't she?"

"I guess," Tory said, standing back as he opened the door for her. "But I like her, anyway."

"Why?"

He was still holding the door, standing there looking at her, and she could feel his glance all the way to her bones.

There was something special about this man. Something compelling. And frightening.

"Because in a time when those guys—your Hawthorne and Melville and Emerson and so on—were writing about witches and wars and big issues, she wrote about ordinary everyday life. Her own life and that of her sisters. She was practical, the way women often are because they have to be. And she was able to take reality and make it palatable. Her writing engaged me as a child and, equally, as an adult."

"I think I prefer books that transform reality," he said, letting go of the door as she started down the hall. "Instead of stories that just present it the way it is."

"Like any good writer, she did both. Her books were based on aspects of her own life, but they weren't autobiographical." Tory shook her head. "I've been to the house where she grew up," she told him. Christine had taken her there—as well as many other places important to American literature. In New England, they'd been right there for the visiting. "It was so...so touching to see things I'd read about. In *Little Women,* one of the heroine's sisters draws all the time, and upstairs in Alcott's home, in this little attic bedroom, there were these incredible pencil sketches along the wall. Louisa's sister had done them."

Tory had treasured that tour. And all the others. For those brief moments history and fantasy had come together.

"You really love this stuff," Ben said, waiting while she unlocked her office door.

Standing there with him right behind her, she wondered why she wasn't feeling the need to run. Usually she couldn't tolerate being so close to a man.

Probably because she was still playing the part of Christine.

"Yeah," she answered. "I really do."

BEN WAS WITH ZACK FOSTER the following evening, driving home from Phoenix. The bed of his truck was filled with Zack's new living-room furniture. As he drove down Main, he saw Christine Evans coming out of Weber's department store. He watched her climb into a brand-new white Ford Mustang. The car seemed to suit her better than the clothes she wore. She never seemed comfortable in them.

But then, she didn't seem comfortable, period.

"Someone you know?" the vet asked, responding to his interest.

"Not exactly," Ben said, pulling his gaze away, refusing to look in his rearview mirror to see which direction Christine had taken. "She's just my English professor."

Zack frowned. "I don't think I've ever seen her before."

"She's new to town."

"She's gorgeous," Zack said, his voice appreciative. "Not that I'm noticing," he added.

"How long ago did your wife leave?" Ben asked, glad to change the subject. Zack had told him, when Ben had stopped in at the vet's to pick up more puppy food for Buddy, that he was having to refurnish his house after his divorce. That was when Ben had offered the use of his truck to pick up Zack's new furniture.

"Six months."

Using the rearview mirror, Ben surveyed the couch and chairs in the back of the truck. "You been sitting on the floor all this time?"

"I haven't been home long enough to sit anywhere."

Ben could understand that. After Mary had left, taking Alex with her, Ben hadn't been able to sit still, either. Though they'd never been in any one apartment for long—Mary had always found some reason or other to be dissatisfied with what his income could provide—there'd still been Alex's laughter bouncing off whatever walls were surrounding them.

"You seeing anyone?" Ben asked. *He* had no interest whatsoever in complicating his life again, but Zack seemed like a man who'd enjoy women. Tall, blond, athletic-looking, the guy probably had women following him in droves.

"Nope," Zack said. "I've been too busy at the clinic. Cassie and I are initiating a national pet-therapy program in universities across the country, and I've been doing a lot of traveling, though not nearly as much as she has."

"I don't imagine there're lots to choose from in a town this size, anyway," Ben commented. The thought pleased him.

"Not many I've noticed." Zack grinned. "But I'm not looking, either. Marriage isn't all it's cracked up to be. I'm in no hurry to put myself through it again."

"Know what you mean."

"You been married?" The vet glanced over at Ben.

"Yeah."

"How long?"

"Eight years."

"Six, here." Zack sent him a purely male look of commiseration. "Eight years," he repeated. "You must have married young."

"I was eighteen. Just finishing high school. I traded my education for a couple of dead-end jobs that allowed me to support my wife."

Zack whistled, motioning for Ben to turn. "It's the last house on the right," he said. And then he added, "She must've been some looker to get her hooks into you that deep."

"Yeah," Ben said. Mary had been beautiful, but it wasn't Mary who'd hooked him.

It was Alex.

CHAPTER FOUR

ALEX SANDERS wondered how far Shelter Valley was from California. She didn't know what streets she had to take, but she might have to walk there.

"Ahhh!" she cried out when the next blow hit her back. She bit her lip. But she didn't cry. She was a big girl now. Daddy had said so the last time he sneaked a phone call to her at this man's place.

One more blow and Alex huddled in the corner. Her lip was bleeding now from biting it. And her back hurt so bad she thought it might be broken.

"Never, ever lie to me again," the man said.

"I won't," Alex whispered. She'd try her best not to. She just wasn't sure how she could stop doing something she *wasn't* doing. How could she promise not to lie again when she hadn't lied in the first place?

She thought of the phone number she had hidden in the pocket of her Cabbage Patch doll. Somehow she was going to have to call Daddy. He'd know the answer. He was her real daddy and he knew everything.

This other man who hit her—Mommy kept telling her to call *him* Daddy.

But she wouldn't. Not ever. No matter what he did to her.

One more blow landed on her bottom when she wasn't looking.

And Alex started to cry.

TORY WAS IN Christine's office after her last class on Friday, double-checking to make sure she'd done everything she'd needed to. And feeling relieved that she'd made it through her second week as a teacher. There'd been no uprisings in any of her classes.

She had a few telephone calls to return—one about an assessment committee Christine had been chosen to sit in on, a student who'd missed class, and Phyllis. She also had a roster to update.

And she had a permanent knot in her stomach.

Yet, as she looked back over the past two weeks, she had to smile. She hadn't been half-bad. What was more, during those moments when she'd forgotten who she really was, she'd actually enjoyed herself. She'd always known she loved literature. Reading it. Studying it. Discussing it. She'd just never known how much she liked teaching, too.

"Come in," she called when a knock sounded at the door.

Her stomach flip-flopped when Ben Sanders entered. The man was definitely something to look at. Six feet tall, with his curly dark hair and big brown eyes, he'd probably led more than one woman astray.

But not this woman.

Dropping his backpack on the floor, he sank into the chair across from her desk. Tory stiffened.

"I just stopped by to let you know I sent off the paper this morning."

"Oh!" She smiled. "Good." Though she tried to keep it in place, she could feel her smile fading. He could just as easily have given her the news in class that morning. Why was he here? What did he want? What did he know?

"Thanks for the suggestion."

"There's no guarantee anything will come of it," she felt compelled to warn him.

"Don't worry, Teach." He grinned. "I gave up on guarantees a long time ago."

"I'm impressed, you know," she said, thinking like a teacher—and suddenly horrified when she heard how the words sounded. She *wasn't* a teacher; she was Tory Evans, failure and fraud.

"Oh?" He gazed over her shoulder at the window behind her desk.

"You not only read the assignments, you think about them."

"I'm here to learn."

"I can't imagine how much time you must spend on homework if you do for all your classes what you do for mine."

Ben leaned forward, his elbows on his knees. "I have the time." He was looking at her again, and the genuine niceness in his eyes, the ease, relaxed her a tiny bit.

"You're not working?"

Shaking his head, he smiled, almost apologetically. "I got a loan, at least for this first semester, so I could concentrate fully on my studies."

"You're older than most of the students in the freshman class," Tory said, though she knew she shouldn't have.

This conversation was traveling places it mustn't go. There was no place in her life for personal conversation between her and a man. Whoever he was.

But for some reason, he was on her mind often....

And there was a big solid desk between them.

"I worked for a number of years after high school," he said.

"Doing what?" It shouldn't have mattered. Shouldn't have interested her.

He shrugged and Tory noticed the breadth of his shoulders. In her fantasy world, they would have been shoulders to cry on, to offer protection. To make her feel safe. In the here and now, the real world, his strength and maleness made her uncomfortable.

"Whatever would pay the rent," he said. "I worked for a moving company in Flagstaff during the day for most of those years, and usually had another job at night. Working on cars, on loading docks, in a grocery store. Even did some construction work on weekends."

The heroes in her mind were always hard workers. Not always rich, but hard workers. Money didn't impress Tory. It couldn't buy anything that mattered.

"I'm surprised, then, that you didn't have enough money saved to pay for college."

She had no idea where her impertinence was coming from. Or her nosiness, but as he sat there looking at her, he seemed to invite the questions.

"I had a wife who liked to spend the money before I managed to earn it."

Her breath caught as she glanced at his left hand. "You're married?"

He shook his head. "Not anymore."

"Oh."

Sitting up, he frowned. "Before you go getting any ideas, she left me, not the other way around."

"I wasn't getting ideas." Okay, maybe she had been. Men deserted women all the time. Why should he be any different?

"Guess I'd better go and let you get back to whatever you were doing," he said, standing. He slid his backpack onto one shoulder.

Tory stood, too, feeling at too much of a disadvantage remaining seated. "Thanks for coming by," she said. When she realized how much she meant the simple words, she added, "To let me know about the submission. I'll keep my fingers crossed for you."

"Thanks."

He turned and left, but not before he'd sent her another of those odd smiles that confused her. Scared her.

He'd smiled the same way that first day of class. Almost as though he was reassuring her, offering her a kindness she hardly dared to recognize.

It had to stop.

"I'M SURE DR. PARSONS and his wife don't want to be bothered with me," Tory said later that evening as Phyllis drove them up the mountain toward the president's beautiful home. "The invitation to dinner was for you."

Phyllis, already sweating in her sleeveless yellow cotton shirt, threw her a sideways glance. "It was for both of us."

"Why would they want to spend one of their few free evenings with me?"

"Why wouldn't they, Tory?" Phyllis asked, her voice serious. "You're a delightful woman with compassion and insight. You have a sense of humor—when you let yourself relax—and intelligent things to say."

Tory smiled, in spite of herself. "You've sure managed to project a lot of things onto me that were never there before." Fantasies were nice, but in the long run they hurt.

"I don't think so," Phyllis said. She slowed as she rounded a curb. Tory studied the saguaro cacti standing erect and proud just a few feet from the drive. "The old man of the desert," Phyllis had told her that type of cactus was called. Tory preferred to think of it as an old woman. A grandmother, stalwart and stoic, who'd survive until the end.

"Okay, for expediency's sake, we'll pretend that the way you describe me has some truth in it. But Dr. Parsons and his wife are expecting someone else—Christine. A confident, accomplished woman. Not *me*." she shuddered. "It makes me nervous that they'd want me here." She watched as the house grew closer and closer. It was beautiful with its mostly glass walls, reminding Tory of a place Bruce owned in the Poconos.

She'd almost killed herself there once. Or at least planned to do it. Until she'd thought of Christine. Then, as always, she'd found the strength to endure.

"You don't think they suspect anything, do you?" she finally asked, heart pounding.

"No!" Phyllis said, taking her hand off the wheel long enough to squeeze Tory's.

Tory wasn't used to the contact. Christine had never been much of a toucher.

"Will was really taken with Christine," Phyllis told her. "Though he only met her once, spoke with her maybe a handful of times, something about her seemed to reach him. I'm sure he just has an interest in getting to know her—you—better."

"Thank you," Tory said, swallowing with difficulty.

"For what?"

"I don't know," Tory answered honestly. "Keeping Christine alive, I guess."

"You do that all by yourself, honey," Phyllis said. "She's so much a part of you, so much inside you, that just having you around is a comfort to me."

They were approaching the house, and Tory wondered if she'd underdressed in spite of Phyllis's assurances to the contrary. Had she been with Bruce, the simple twill shorts and cotton blouse would have been an embarrassment. How would Will and Becca Parsons react to her appearance? She shook her head. She had to think about something besides the intimidating people she was about to see.

"I've been thinking about looking for an apartment," she admitted suddenly. She'd been meaning to broach the subject all week, but until now, the time had never been right.

"Why?"

The genuine distress in Phyllis's voice brought warm tears to Tory's eyes.

"Because it's your home and I'm afraid I'm outstaying my welcome."

Parking the car in front of the Parsons home, Phyllis turned off the ignition but left the keys hanging there as she faced Tory. "Listen, I know that someday you're going to be ready to move out, to have your own place, your own life, and when that time comes, I'll help you find just what you want. Until then, please don't even think about going. I love having you there, Tory. After Boston, this town is so quiet I need the company."

Tory swallowed again, her lips cracking into a smile. "You're sure?"

"Absolutely."

Knowing she was exceedingly lucky, Tory followed Phyllis to the door, armed with a little more strength.

She was fully aware of why Phyllis had opened her home to her. And even that made her feel a little better.

Once again, Christine had come through for her.

"YOU WANT TO HOLD her?"

Tory sat back on the couch in the comfortably elegant, glass-walled family room of the Parsons home and shook her head as Becca offered her month-old daughter.

"I've never...I wouldn't know..."

The child terrified her. Babies were far too fragile to be part of Tory's life.

"Come on," Phyllis coaxed, taking little Bethany from Becca's arms. "She's an absolute charmer, and I ought to know. I spent every single day with her until you got here."

"I'm sorry," Tory said, stricken, as she looked from Becca to Phyllis. It had grown increasingly obvious during the course of the evening that the two women had become close friends over the past two months. "I didn't mean to take you away from what you'd normally be doing."

"It's okay," Becca was the one to answer, smiling at Tory. "August was kind of a rough month around here." She stopped, sharing a secret though somewhat sad smile with her husband. He'd just entered the room with a tray of drinks, his protective glance shooting toward his daughter, then to his wife. Tory had been a whole lot more comfortable when it was just the four females in the room. Even with one of them being only a month old.

"I needed a keeper," Becca continued, "and Phyllis was kind enough to volunteer. Nowadays, I have more people around than I know what to do with."

"You reap what you sow, my love," Will said, setting glasses of iced tea down on the coffee table. He'd exchanged the suit he'd worn to work for a pair of denim shorts and a polo shirt. It felt odd to Tory, seeing her boss so casually dressed. Odder still for him and his wife to insist she call them Becca and Will.

Leaving her daughter with Phyllis on the couch, Becca moved to stand beside her husband. They were a striking couple. Wearing a pair of pleated off-white shorts with a tucked-in emerald silk blouse, Becca wasn't as casually dressed as her husband, but she complemented him perfectly.

Tory wondered if the love they exuded was real.

"Becca's the town's go-to person," Phyllis explained. "She runs the town council, every committee that's worthwhile in town, and has time left over to take care of the rest of us."

"I'm not that bad," Becca told Tory wryly.

"Yes, she is," Will inserted, giving his wife a sideways glance that was clearly a special communication between the two of them. "And now that she's a mom, she's thinking about organizing an afternoon social time for mothers with new babies, too, so they can exchange dirty-diaper stories.''

"I am not!" Becca said. "I merely said I can't wait until Sari has her baby so I'll have someone to share colic stories with.''

"Sari's Becca's younger sister," Phyllis informed Tory. "And really, if you ever do need to get something done in this town, Becca's the one to go to. Doesn't matter that she's home with Bethany now. She still manages to make things happen. Still makes it to her council meetings, too. She had that statue of Samuel Montford erected downtown this summer. And after organizing the Save the Youth program for the city's teens, she and her sisters did a load of research and a friend wrote a play for the kids to do depicting the life of the town's founder.''

"Wow."

"It was so good I stayed awake through the whole thing," Will teased.

Despite her general discomfort with men, Tory had liked Will when she'd met him briefly that first day of class. She liked him even more now.

Which made her eager to leave.

"Stop it, you two," Becca said, watching Bethany sleep snugly in Phyllis's arms. "You're going to have Christine thinking I'm an old fusspot.''

Christine.

For a moment there, Tory had forgotten who she was.

"SHE'S NICE," Becca said later that evening as she lay beside Will in their bed, nursing Bethany.

"I told you she is."

"I know." But that was last spring when she and Will had hardly been speaking, when her marriage had been on the brink of collapse and Becca was half out of her mind with fear. And worry. And so in love, in spite of the odd midlife crisis that had caught her and Will unawares.

Will was gazing at Bethany, his eyelids drooping, almost as though he was falling asleep. But Becca knew he wasn't. Not until Bethany was finished and he'd had his chance to burp her and put her back in the cradle at the end of their bed.

"You were right about Christine. Her eyes hold a lot of secrets."

"She looks different than she did last spring— hair short, framing her face, instead of hanging all the way down her back, probably ten or more pounds lighter. But I recognized her instantly by those eyes."

"What do you think put the sadness there?"

"I have no idea," Will said, but she could tell he'd given the matter some thought.

Two months ago Becca would have felt threatened by that. Tonight all she felt was compassion. For the woman she'd once suspected her husband was falling in love with. And for her husband, as well.

He honestly wanted to help Christine Evans and didn't even know if she needed help.

Becca pulled her drowsy baby off her breast, kissed the downy head with the thankful prayer she never forgot to utter and gently handed her to her father. As she did, Becca made a promise to herself that she'd do whatever she could to make Christine Evans's new life a happy one.

"I KNOW IT'S TOO CLICHÉD for words, but can I help you carry those?"

Christine gave a start and dropped the armload of heavy anthologies she clutched as Ben came up behind her late Monday afternoon. They didn't fall neatly, a couple of them opening and landing on splayed pages.

"I'm sorry," he said, on his haunches immediately. "I didn't mean to scare you."

Crouched carefully in her stiff blue suit, Christine gathered her books. Her hand was shaking. With his backpack hanging precariously off one shoulder, he helped her.

"Hasn't anyone ever told you not to come up on a woman from behind?" she asked, smiling at him. But the smile was tremulous, the words a bit forced.

"Probably." Maybe not. He wasn't in the habit of startling women.

He brushed dust off a big black anthology of American poetry. "Now that they're dirty, as well as heavy, may I carry them for you?"

"Oh." Her movements were abrupt as she handed over the volumes she'd rescued. "Sure. Thanks."

"You heading back to your office?"

"Yes."

It was late Monday afternoon. The temperature was nearing a hundred, in spite of the fact that it was officially fall. Ben adjusted his pace to her slower one.

"You have a good weekend?" He'd spent his refusing to think about her, wondering about her personal history, and refusing to think about her some more. In his spare time, he'd studied.

"Yes, I did," she told him, waving as they passed a group of students, her features relaxing. "It was quiet, but that's the way I like things."

"No heavy dates?" Where in hell had that come from?

"I don't date."

A woman after his own heart.

"Not ever? Or not yet, given that you're new to town and haven't had a chance to meet anyone?"

She sent him a glance that put him firmly in his place. "Kind of a personal question to be asking your teacher, isn't it, Ben?"

"Probably."

"How about you? You have a date this weekend?"

Ben bit back a smile. "Nope. I don't date, either."

Christine nodded and they walked in silence for a moment. This was the weirdest experience Ben could remember having. He wasn't pursuing her. He wanted nothing from her. She was obviously uncomfortable around him.

And yet he couldn't stay away from her.

Judging by the number of times she'd looked his way during class, he was guessing she didn't exactly object.

CHAPTER FIVE

AT HOME THAT EVENING, trying to study for an economics exam he had the next day, Ben hollered and threw down his pen.

"That hurt!" he told the beast smiling up at him from beneath the kitchen table. "My toes are not for your consumption."

Buddy's ears dropped at his stern tone, and Ben's anger disappeared.

"Come here, little man," he said, sliding to the floor.

Tennis ball in hand, he engaged the puppy in a game of catch. He'd only been working on this for a week and already Buddy was bringing the ball back to him.

"You're a quick learner, aren't you, Bud?" he praised after the fifth retrieval. Buddy sat, pressing his head into Ben's hand as Ben scratched him behind the ears. "Wanna read some economics for me?"

The phone rang and, jumping up to answer it, he missed Buddy's reply. Other than various utility services and the school—and Zack—there was only one person who had his new telephone number. It was after hours, so no services or school personnel would be calling. And when he and Zack had shot some hoops on Saturday, Zack had mentioned that he was going into Phoenix to visit some friends this evening. He'd invited Ben to join him, have a few beers, relax for a while. Ben had been tempted, but economics had won out.

"Alex?" He picked up the phone on the second ring. "Is that you, honey?"

The operator interrupted, telling him he had a collect call from Ms. Alex Sanders. Would he accept the charge?

Of course he would.

His little girl had used his name, not the bastard's, though Mary had already had it legally changed.

"Daddy?" Her voice almost brought tears to his eyes. He missed her so damn much. "Daddy, it's me, Alex. Can you hear me?"

"I can, sweetie. How are you?"

"Okay, I guess. I called in secret. Mommy said no again."

"Is something wrong, baby?"

"Noooo. Only I want you to live here with me, Daddy. Can't you just ask Mommy if you can have a room, too? We got an extra."

"We've already talked about this, Al," Ben said softly, forcing cheer into his voice. "Your mommy wants you to give your new daddy a chance, and when I'm there, that's too hard for you to do."

"Do you want me to give Pete a chance, too, Daddy?"

If it would make Alex happy? "Yes, I do." The words stuck in his throat. The bastard damn well better love Alex with every sorry bone in his body. She sure as hell wasn't going to get enough caring from her mother.

Silence hung on the line. Ben couldn't bear to waste a single second of the brief time he had to talk with his little girl. "You'll try really hard for me, won't you, Al?"

"Okay. But…"

"What, baby?"

"Daddy, do you know how to not lie again when you didn't lie?"

"What?"

"Because it's real important, Daddy. *Real* important."

What? Ben's stomach tensed at the strange tone in Alex's voice. He'd never heard it before. Had no idea what it meant. He knew her tired cry, her hurt cry. He knew her happy laugh and her faking-it laugh. But he didn't know what she was trying to tell him now.

"Do you know, Daddy?"

Ben scrambled, trying furiously to translate the question into something that made sense.

"If you don't lie to begin with, baby, then you don't have to worry about not lying again," he finally told her.

"Are you sure, Daddy?"

Ben paced his kitchen, the mobile phone to his ear. "I'm sure."

"Promise?"

"Yes."

She was quiet again and Ben couldn't help wondering how she'd managed to sneak in the call.

"Where's Mommy?"

"She and Pete went across the road."

And left Alex alone? At night? "What are they doing there?"

"I dunno. They've got friends there. I'm supposed to be asleep."

Cold and sick, Ben stayed on the phone while he had Alex take the mobile unit and go check the doors and windows. Then, making her promise to go right to bed and to sleep—knowing that if she was sleeping she wouldn't be able to feel scared or lonely—he finally hung up the phone.

Mary was going to be hearing from him whether she liked it or not.

TUESDAY AFTERNOON on his way home, Ben took a detour to visit his great-grandfather, wondering what the best time was to catch his ex-wife without her new husband around. They were having one of Arizona's rare cloudy days, and he was eager to be outside, soaking it up, at least long enough to calm him for that phone call. He also wanted to share the good news about his first-ever college exam, and his long-dead ancestor was the only one he could think of who'd appreciate his accomplishment. He didn't have his grade yet, but he *knew* he'd done well, and the whole experience hadn't been nearly as intimidating as he'd expected. Pulling his truck to the curb, he noticed a white Mustang parked a couple of spaces over and thought of Christine. Ever since he'd found out what she drove, he always thought of her when he saw a Mustang.

He looked around for her, just in case the car was hers. Not that he'd seek her out even if he knew where she was. He had nothing to say to her outside of class. No reason to know what she might be doing downtown. What shops she might frequent.

Still, it didn't hurt to look. To be on his guard.

The car was empty, the area surrounding it deserted—much to his disappointment. Shaking his head at his adolescent behavior, Ben headed for the statue. Just a quick silent chat with his great-grandfather and then he was going home to hit redial all night if that was what it took to get hold of Mary. Pete be damned.

Ben had supported Alex for the first six years of her life while that bastard sat in a prison cell for stealing cars. Lots of cars. Ben had not only worked years off his life to support Alex, he'd raised her. He'd taught her the difference between right and wrong, shown her how to be sensitive to other people's needs, potty-trained her. He'd loved her.

He loved her still.

Christine was sitting on a bench in front of his statue.

Great. The woman was going to think he was stalking her.

And she was trespassing at *his* statue.

"What are you doing here?" he asked her, taking the offensive before she could accuse him of following her.

"Sitting," she said. At least she didn't jump. Or drop the book she'd been reading. "Phyllis, Dr. Langford, is getting her hair done. Her car's in for a tune-up, so I drove today."

"You two live close by?" She looked different. Younger.

It didn't take long to figure out why. She was wearing an expensive-looking pair of shorts and a sleeveless blouse. And a pair of casual, though high-heeled, sandals. Much more relaxed attire than he was used to seeing her in.

"We're sharing a house on Elm Street," Christine said. "The house is Dr. Langford's, actually. I'm staying with her until I find something of my own."

"You two know each other from before?"

Christine nodded, arms folded in front of her, the book she'd been reading closed on her lap. "We met at Boston College."

"As students?" Hands in the pockets of his denim shorts, he placed a foot on one end of the white cement bench.

Shaking her head, Christine looked at his foot. "As teachers."

He was making her uncomfortable again, and for the life of him, he couldn't understand why. Girls had always run to him for security or advice, for help out of whatever trouble they'd gotten themselves into. Until now, they'd never run *from* him.

Not that Christine was running. He just had a feeling that she wanted to.

"Are you this tense all the time," he asked, "or is it just me?"

"I'm not tense." Throwing up her hands to reinforce her denial, she knocked her purse to the ground.

Ben picked it up and gave it back to her. Her fingers, as they brushed his, were shaky. And soft.

"I don't bite," he muttered.

"Of course you don't." She laughed stiffly.

Ben sat down. Christine scooted over, ostensibly to make room for him, in spite of the two feet he'd left between them. If she moved again, she'd fall right off the end.

"I've never hurt a woman in my life," he said.

"I didn't think you had."

He didn't know why her reaction bothered him so much; he just knew he couldn't let it go.

"Do I make you nervous for some reason?"

"No!" She was staring at the statue of his great-grandfather. "Uh, maybe. Yes, maybe you do."

Ben frowned, trying to figure out how he might have treated her differently from how he'd treated anyone else.

"You're my student," she said, her voice relaxing some. "I'm sure it's not proper that we be—"

"Friends?"

"Right." She glanced over at him quickly and then away. "Friends."

"Is that what's happening here?" he asked, suddenly as intent as she. "Are we becoming friends?"

"I hardly know you."

"Would you like to?" Why was her answer so important?

"Sure. Of course." Her arms were folded around herself again as she stared at the statue in front of them. "I don't know." She looked in his direction. "Probably not."

She didn't convince him. "Because I'm in your class?"

"Montford has a strict code of ethics, and I know I read something about improper behavior between students and teachers."

"Our friendship doesn't have to be improper." Ben wanted to turn toward her, to look at her face while they were talking, to see what expressions were accompanying her words, but the conversation was too important to risk making her run.

"I'm not a young college kid," he reminded her. "I'd guess I'm as old as you are, or close to it."

She didn't say anything.

"I'm twenty-six, by the way."

"Oh."

"How old are you, Christine?"

"Thirty."

"See?" He glanced at her and then at his great-grandfather again. "Hardly any difference at all."

He'd guessed she was a little younger than that, but he'd never been a good judge of age. Especially with women. Besides, sometimes when he met her eyes in class, they looked ancient. Yes, he decided, she could easily be thirty.

She was quiet again. But she didn't make any excuse to leave. That had to mean something.

His great-grandfather stared right back at him, sculpted stone eyes filled with compassion, almost as though he could hear this strange conversation—and understood.

Ben wished *he* understood. He had no idea why he was even sitting there.

"Have you been here before?" Ben finally asked, gesturing at the statue.

Christine nodded, tapping her fingers on her book. "Phyllis brought me on Sunday. We were at dinner Friday night with the woman who had this piece commissioned last spring."

"He's Shelter Valley's founder," Ben said.

What woman had had a statue of his ancestor commissioned? And why?

"I know. Becca Parsons and her family researched his biography all last winter. And a friend of theirs, Martha Moore, wrote a play, which was put on by Shelter Valley teenagers on the Fourth of July, the day the statue was unveiled. I guess there was a big write-up in the paper, too."

Ben sat up. If there was a write-up in the paper, he should still be able to get a copy of it at the library. He'd been planning to do his own research once he got settled in school and had some extra time. He knew about the early years of his great-grandfather's life, but his knowledge ended abruptly—with the day his grandmother had left home.

Part of his reason for coming to Shelter Valley was to find out about his family. Find out who he was.

She nodded, fingers lying still across the book.

"I don't know about you, but I've never lived in a community like this," he went on, "one where everyone knows everyone else, and more, watches out for everyone else."

"And everyone else's kids, too," Christine said, smiling. "I never have, either."

"I find it pretty incredible."

"I do, too." Her words were so soft he barely heard them.

"A bit like I've arrived on another planet," he said.

"I know what you mean." She nodded, looked over at him. "Everyone knows who I am, but I can hardly keep track of the kids in my classes, let alone every other person I pass on the street."

"Kind of helps having an influx of nearly six thousand students, though, doesn't it? We don't stand out quite so much."

"Except that most of them live in the dorms...."

"But some get jobs in town."

"They're younger than we are. We still stand out."

For a very brief moment, they connected again, just as they had that first day of class.

What the hell was happening to him?

His gaze darted away from her, landing back on the statue. "He's my great-grandfather."

"Really?"

For a diversionary tactic, his ploy had worked. Except that now she knew something he'd been planning to keep to himself. At least for a while—until he'd completely soaked up the feeling of Shelter Valley, made this place his own.

Ben nodded. "My grandmother was his daughter."

"You're related to Samuel Montford?" She was looking at him fully now.

"I am."

"I don't believe this! Becca was just telling us the other night that the only Montfords still alive were Sam's namesake, a great-grandson who left Shelter Valley more than ten years ago, and his parents who have a home in Shelter Valley, but have lived in Europe for more than a year."

He had a cousin? An aunt and uncle? Ben's heartbeat quickened. He had *family?* Legitimate family of his own?

"Where'd Sam go?" He had a cousin. Maybe even close to him in age.

"Apparently no one knows for sure. They tried to locate him, to ask him to come back for the dedication, but they couldn't find him. I gather he left town in something of a disgrace. It had to do with a broken marriage, I think. His wife is still here in town. They mentioned her name, but I don't remember it. Sam moves around a lot."

Ben had a cousin.

Christine looked over at him again. "So if you're a Montford, how come nobody knows about you?"

She was more at ease than he'd ever seen her.

"My grandmother left Shelter Valley when she was fourteen."

"Old Sam's daughter! She disappeared in the desert. They figured she got lost, died, and then wild animals got her remains."

"That's what they thought?"

Christine shrugged. "Becca was just telling us about it the other night. The sheriff and his men searched everywhere for her and eventually concluded that she must be dead. They held a funeral for her, erected a headstone that's still standing out at the cemetery. But apparently, no matter what people said, Sam never believed his daughter had died." She stopped, staring at the statue of his great-grandfather, her eyes wide as she shook her head. "It's hard to believe, you know, that a man could love his daughter so much."

Thinking of Alex, it wasn't hard to believe at all. Ben watched Christine closely. What kind of life had she led that she'd find a father's love so foreign?

"He was the only one, though." She continued her narrative, and Ben left his questions for another time. "Becca said even the girl's mother was convinced she'd met with a tragic fate in the desert. Sam spent the rest of his life waiting for her return."

The oddest feeling came over Ben, as though two parts of himself had just met for the first time. Unconnected halves becoming one whole. His blood ran cold and then hot. He'd always heard about those later years second-hand, through his father and from his grandmother's point of view.

"She missed him all her life."

"Why didn't she ever get in touch with him, then? Where'd she go? Why didn't she come home?"

Ben turned, his arm along the back of the bench as he faced her. "She fell in love with a Hopi Indian she'd met out riding in the desert. They used to meet secretly, in a cave they found halfway up the mountain on the south end of town."

"But Becca said that Sam had lived with the Indians—when he first came out West from Boston."

"That's what my grandmother told my father when he was little."

"So why couldn't she just tell her father she'd fallen in love? Why did she have to hide?"

Christine was like a different person, relaxed, completely alive.

"Did Becca Parsons tell you about Sam's first marriage?" he asked, eager to continue the conversation, to be able to share something that, until then, he'd guarded so carefully. "The way it ended?"

Her brows coming together as she thought, Christine nodded. "He married a black woman, didn't he?"

"That's right," Ben murmured.

"And people, his family and friends, went a little crazy."

"Slavery was still legal back then. They might have lived in the North, but that didn't mean interracial marriages were accepted."

"They had a baby, and one day while his wife was out walking with her son, they were both attacked. Killed." Christine shuddered.

If she'd been any other woman, Ben would have put his arm around her, touched her face, something to bring her back, to reassure her that it was only a story from a bygone day.

"You can see why his daughter didn't dare tell him she wanted to enter into an interracial marriage of her own."

"But..."

"She tried once," Ben said, relaying the story he'd been told when, as a young boy, he'd visited the reservation where his father had been born and raised. Some of the old people had still remembered his grandmother. "But she only got as far as saying they were friends. Samuel forbade her to see him anymore and then spent hours lecturing her on the proper behavior of a young white girl, whom she should and shouldn't see as she prepared herself for marriage."

"And he thought that was it? That she didn't see the Indian again?"

Ben nodded. "She even tried to do as he'd ordered. For a time. But she was so much in love and kept riding out to their cave, just hoping he'd be there."

"And he was."

"Yeah." And Ben had never been sure that was a good thing. "She and her...friend eventually became lovers out in their cave, and she got pregnant. She knew the knowledge would kill her father, that if it didn't initially, it would eventually as he worried himself to death about her safety and the safety of her baby. Her Hopi lover—"

"Your grandfather..." He saw the truth dawn in her widened eyes.

"—insisted that she come home with him, be his wife, live with his tribe and raise their child as one of his people. She was young, in love. And scared to death."

"She went with him," Christine whispered.

"Yes."

"And his people were cruel to her, weren't they."

"No," Ben said, shaking his head as he looked once again at the statue of Samuel Montford.

"She was happy with them?"

"Except for missing her family in Shelter Valley, she was very happy. She'd always intended to come back once enough time had passed to assure her father that what had happened to his first wife and son would not happen to her and her baby."

"So what stopped her?"

"She got a fever and died. She was only twenty-four."

"How sad!"

Yeah. And the rest of the story didn't get any better. Because as it turned out, her father's fears had not been as unfounded as she'd hoped. Her husband's people might have been willing to accept a half-breed, but the rest of the world—even neighboring tribes—hadn't been so charitable. Ben's father had spent his entire life running from who he was—and what he wasn't.

He'd married a white woman, had a son, but he'd been unable to live in their world, to accept the prejudices he too often came up against as an Indian in a white man's world.

And he wanted more than he could find with his father's people.

He'd wanted more than he could find…anywhere.

CHAPTER SIX

"So this is why you came to Shelter Valley," Christine said softly, glancing from Ben to the statue standing proudly in front of them.

"Partly," Ben said, feeling raw suddenly, as though he'd given up far more of himself than he should have. "The university played a big role in my decision, too."

They were the wrong words to say, reminding Christine of his place in her life. Her place in his.

"Now don't go becoming all Ms. Teacher on me again," he said, poking her arm with his elbow.

She straightened, and her glance touched him, then skittered away. "I *am* your teacher."

"I'm not arguing that point, and I promise not to pressure you to give me good grades...." He hoped a little humor would leaven the situation.

"Judging by the couple of papers you've already turned in, you're going to earn those all by yourself." She spoke seriously, apparently unaware that he'd been joking. She was looking at the ground, pushing a rock around with the toe of her sandal.

"So what's the harm in two people who have something in common—a displaced feeling in a town where most of the permanent residents know each other—keeping company now and then?''

Though she didn't move, he could feel her escaping him and wished he hadn't pushed her. He had no idea why he'd even made the suggestion, since he had no desire to ''keep company'' with anyone. For a long time to come.

''I—''

''Tell you what,'' he interrupted. ''Why don't we just let it be for now, huh?'' Maybe they'd run into each other once in a while—or maybe not. ''I don't have room in my life for complications, either.''

She gave a stilted nod. He waited for her to make some excuse, to get up and leave. She didn't. He thought about doing so himself.

''How come *you* chose Shelter Valley?'' he asked, instead.

Hand fumbling with the ends of her shoulder-length hair, Christine answered, her voice tighter than before. ''I wanted a change of pace from Boston, and this position was available, Montford has an impeccable reputation, good advancement opportunities, and here I am.''

''What about Dr. Langford?''

''I was speaking with Dr. Parsons on the phone one day after I was hired, and he happened to mention that he was looking for a psychology professor. My-I, uh, thought of Phyllis immediately. She's had a hard time letting go of her ex-husband, and the change of scenery seemed like a good idea for her, too.''

She hadn't met his eyes as she spoke, but at least she'd raised her head, gazing out at the park. "Besides," she muttered, "coming out here alone seemed kind of scary. Having a f-friend along made it an adventure."

Ben had been reading what people *weren't* saying his entire life. With his father, it helped him stay a step ahead of conflict.

And there was definitely more to Christine's story. He could feel it, could sense the gaps.

But that was fine. Her life wasn't his business. He and Christine were no more than a teacher and student who ran across each other occasionally.

"Do you mind if I tell Becca—" Christine motioned to the statue of his great-grandfather "—about your relationship to him?"

Ben's stomach tightened. He'd learned a long time ago to keep his family history to himself. Other than his dark hair, he didn't carry any outward signs of his Indian heritage. Life had taught him to go with that.

"I wouldn't even ask, except that she really seems to care about him," she said, her eyes understanding as they finally met Ben's. "You'd think he was *her* great-grandfather."

That might be, but...

"You wouldn't have to worry," Christine assured him, "Becca's wonderful, not the gossipy sort at all."

Uncomfortable, Ben had a feeling he wasn't the

only one who'd developed the ability to read between the lines of what people said.

And because he couldn't have her doing that,
couldn't let her know she'd read him right, he
shrugged as he stood.

"Sure, tell her," he said. "I don't mind at all."

But of course he did.

TORY DIDN'T RETURN to the beauty shop to pick up
Phyllis. She'd told Phyllis she planned to run to the
drugstore for a couple of things and come right back.
Phyllis paid her bill, tried to be cordial and polite
as she waved goodbye and rushed out of the shop.

Tory's car was still in the parking space, just as
they'd left it when they arrived. It was empty.

Heart beating, Phyllis glanced up and down the
street. *Please let her be okay.*

She couldn't see Tory anywhere.

Could Bruce really find her here? Was his influence that extensive? Christine had been convinced
that Tory would be safe here. But Phyllis knew that
Tory herself believed it was only a matter of time
before Bruce found her.

Tory wasn't in the drugstore. Nor was she in
Weber's. Or at the Valley Diner having a glass of
iced tea.

Bruce thought Tory was dead. He wouldn't be
looking for her, would he? Unless he'd come to see
Christine for some reason.

And found out who really died.

Oh. God.

Every breath a labor, Phyllis hurried up and down both sides of Main Street, searching everywhere. She'd only known her a few short weeks, but already felt as though Tory was the little sister she'd never had. In that regard, she'd stepped into Christine's shoes as easily as if she'd worn them all her life.

Phyllis stopped abruptly as she crossed the far edge of the town square. Tory was sitting on a bench by the statue of Samuel Montford. *With a man.*

Tory wouldn't sit and talk casually with a man. She'd excuse herself and move away. She'd even felt uncomfortable the other night with Will Parsons, and he was not only nonthreatening, he'd treated Tory in a gracious, welcoming way.

Yet spending an evening in his presence, with Phyllis and his wife for company, had exhausted Tory.

So why was she sitting there now? And well past the time she was supposed to be back at the hairdressing salon?

Phyllis's heart started to pound. Could the man be Bruce?

And if he was, what should she do? Make herself known? Demand that he leave Tory alone?

Or would she be better able to help Tory if the man didn't know who she was, what she looked like?

Who was she fooling?

If Bruce had the ability to trace Tory to Shelter

Valley, he'd know exactly who Phyllis was, too. Probably had an entire dossier on her.

She couldn't let him get away with this.

She marched right up to them.

"I don't know who you think you are, you bastard, but you touch one hair on her head and I'll kill you myself."

"Uh, Phyllis—"

"No, Christine! I won't let him do this to you. I—"

"Phyllis!" The urgent note in Tory's voice registered at about the same instant the man's astonished and thoroughly confused expression did.

"Do what?" the man asked.

"I'd just told Phyllis on the way into town that one of the guys at the hardware store has been after me all week to go out with him. He won't take no for an answer. I'm sure Phyllis thought you were him."

Phyllis was impressed with her friend's quick recovery, but she shouldn't have been surprised. Tory had survived four years of Bruce's tyranny. She'd buried her dead sister in a strange town with only herself to rely on. And then driven cross-country to take her sister's place—and begin a deception of staggering complexity.

The woman was a survivor. And smart. Loyal, too.

Phyllis was going to have to calm down. She hadn't realized how much this whole situation was getting to her. Tory's future mattered so much. And she'd almost gone and blown things for her.

"Phyllis Langford, meet Ben Sanders," Tory said as politely as any society matron. Standing, she took refuge slightly behind Phyllis.

"Glad to meet you," Phyllis said, her mind racing. Who *was* this man?

Could Tory possibly be interested in him?

"Nice to meet you, too," the man said. His hand, when he shook Phyllis's, was warm, gentle—yet firm.

"Ben's in my 9 a.m. American Lit class," Tory said.

And Tory had been sitting on this bench of her own free will, talking to him.

Phyllis shook the man's hand a little more vigorously, more thankful than he'd ever know to make his acquaintance. Tory had been talking to him. Amazing. Wonderful. A hopeful sign?

Except—Phyllis reined in her thoughts as she and Tory told Ben goodbye and headed back to the Mustang—even if Tory was able to recover enough to actually be able to have a relationship, she wasn't free to do so. She was living a lie.

Something neither of them had considered when they'd formulated this plan.

They'd just had a very close call—a lesson to both of them about the little game they were playing.

IT WAS ALMOST MIDNIGHT before Ben got an answer. He'd been dialing his ex-wife's number every half hour since seven, his mind seesawing back and forth between Alex and Christine while he listened to the constant ringing on the other end of the line.

"Mary, it's Ben," he said without preamble when she finally answered.

"Why are you calling me?"

"We have to talk."

"There's nothing more to say. The divorce is final, Ben. It's over."

"Don't hang up!" Ben said quickly. "It's about Alex."

"Pete's her father, Ben. She doesn't need you anymore." The barb hit its mark.

"I think she does."

"Playing hero again?"

"I called last night." Ben fibbed to protect his little girl. There was no telling what they'd do to her if they knew she'd called him.

"I told you not to."

"I know," Ben said. "But that's not the point. It was late, Mary. She was home alone."

"So?"

"She's only seven years old!"

"For God's sake, Ben, we were just across the street and Alex was in bed."

"She didn't sound happy."

"How can she be, with you confusing her like this? Stay out of her life, Ben. Let Alex get to know Pete, to love him as she should love her father."

"As she loves me."

"*He's* her father."

Another dig. She was two for two.

"Just promise me you won't leave her alone anymore, especially at night," Ben said.

He couldn't shake the unidentifiable tone he'd heard in Alex's voice the night before. Couldn't do what Mary wanted and just disappear. He'd spent seven years loving that little girl.

"I don't have to promise you anything," she said irritably. "Not anymore."

Ben took a deep breath. "I'm worried about Alex."

"Pete's gonna to be home anytime now, and I don't want him to find me talking to you."

"I promise not to call if you promise not to leave her by herself anymore," he said.

She sighed. "You swear?"

"Yes." But only because he knew Alex would call him if she needed to.

"All right."

Ben wasn't sure how much weight the promise carried, given Mary's track record for breaking every promise she'd ever made to him. But at least she knew he was still watching out for Alex, that he wasn't willing just to go away. He hoped the knowledge would make her a little more conscientious.

At the moment, with his hands tied by the California legal system, it was the best he could do.

AS SHE PULLED into the faculty parking lot the second Friday in October, Tory glanced in her rearview mirror before shutting off the Mustang's engine. She always looked behind her first, ensured that no one was lurking. Came from being hunted, having someone approach her from behind as she opened her car door and having no way to escape. Making sure there was always an escape route had become second nature to her.

A car pulled into a parking spot several rows over. A practical-looking sedan, the sort a teacher would drive—except that it was dark. Very few people who lived in Arizona drove dark cars. Tory waited, her hand on the gearshift, ready to throw the car back in drive. There wasn't a car in front of her; she could drive straight through and—

"Stop it!" she admonished herself.

No one was coming for her. Tory was dead.

Checking in her rearview mirror again, she finally turned off the ignition. If she wasn't careful, she'd be certifiable in no time.

Not to mention late for class.

She hadn't seen anyone get out of the dark car. A fellow faculty member would have gotten out, gone to whatever building on campus housed his office or his class. But if someone was after her, he'd be sitting in that car—watching her.

Heart pounding, she tried to make out the interior of the car through the rows of vehicles. The familiar claustrophobic panic took hold of her. Was that a shadow in the car? Two shadows? Bruce's men usually traveled in pairs.

What were they waiting for?

If they were there for her, why didn't they come out? Or had someone sneaked up behind her car, beneath the mirror view? As she'd grown wiser, so had her hired captors.

Tory looked around desperately, hoping to see someone she knew, a security guard, a faculty member, even a secretary. Anyone else, anyone at all.

The parking lot was deserted. She should never have used the back lot. But it was closer to her office building, which meant spending less time out in the open, exposed on campus, but sometimes, like today, it was deserted. With shaking hands, she shoved the key back in the ignition. She had to get out of there. Go—

"Stop. Oh, please stop," she begged. "Just let me live."

There was no one out to get her except the demons in her own mind. Tory was dead.

She drew in a shuddering breath, gathered up her leather satchel and purse, placed her finger firmly over the trigger on her can of pepper spray and got out of the car. But not without a quick glance behind her. She could never be too sure.

Practically running to her 9 a.m. class, Tory told herself the rush was to avoid being late. And maybe it was, at least partially. But she'd never run like this—as though the devil was on her heels—just because she was late.

She made it to the room as the preceding class was dismissed. Slowing her step, she took a deep breath, mentally collected herself and walked to the front of the room.

She could do this. She knew the routine. She was fine.

If you could call letting panic propel you fine.

Tory removed the books and papers she needed for class from her satchel and mentally reviewed the lesson ahead of her. She would be introducing Henry Wadsworth Longfellow. With her breathing almost normal again—although her heart rate wasn't as quick to recover—Tory methodically coached herself back to relative sanity.

As of that afternoon, she'd been in Shelter Valley a month. In the past couple of years, Tory had never stayed in any one place for more than a few weeks. That was all her panic meant, she told herself. Her instincts didn't know yet that she was safe in this place, that she was no longer on the run.

"You okay?" Ben Sanders was standing by her desk, blocking her view of the classroom.

"Yes," she said, fidgeting with her notes. "Fine."

"You sure?" he asked softly.

He didn't touch her, didn't move, yet he compelled Tory to look up at him. In his eyes was the most comforting mixture of understanding and compassion Tory had ever seen. It took her breath away.

He couldn't know. Had no way of knowing.

"Yes," she answered him again, surprised to find that she was almost telling the truth. "I'm fine."

Knocking once on the top of her desk, Ben gave her a last searching look and proceeded to his seat.

"Ben?" Tory called after him.

"Yeah?" He turned to face her.

"Can you stay after class today, just for a minute?"

"Of course." She liked the way he didn't even hesitate to do as she asked, yet at the same time, she felt threatened by his easy compliance. She couldn't have him wanting anything from her in return.

"I spoke with Becca Parsons and I have a message for you," she told him, ensuring that he didn't get the wrong idea.

Ben nodded and continued on to his seat, once again a student like all the rest.

A couple of weeks ago he'd asked Tory for her friendship. For a split second there, she'd been tempted to give it to him. But only until she'd remembered that she didn't have anything to give.

Her life was a lie.

She was an imposter.

Tory Evans was dead.

CHAPTER SEVEN

"TELL ME WHY you like 'The Children's Hour' so much," Ben said, walking with Tory toward her office. "It's not considered one of Longfellow's major poems, but it's obviously special to you."

By the time she'd finished answering questions immediately after class, another class had been preparing to start and there hadn't been time to speak with Ben in private.

She had a message for him from Becca Parsons, just as she'd said. And a favor to ask. Not something that could be done with his fellow students milling about. So she'd asked him to walk along with her.

"Special to me?" she asked, relaxing a bit as she accepted his presence.

He'd taken to walking Tory to her office almost every day after their class. He'd explained that he had another class in a building on the same side of campus the following hour. During these brief walks, they'd fallen into the habit of discussing whatever had been the class topic that day, and Tory had begun to enjoy the stolen moments. Today, however, had been the first time she'd been the one to suggest he accompany her.

Because she was on a mission for Becca Parsons. Not because she was still jittery from this morning's episode in the parking lot and wanted the reassurance of his company.

"Special to you," Ben repeated.

"How do you know it *is* special to me?" she asked, careful as usual to keep enough distance between them that they never touched as they walked. "I have to cover a lot of ground in this class—not every poem or story is going to be among my personal favorites."

"Ah, but this one really is, isn't it?" he insisted, grinning at her.

"What makes you so sure?" She grinned back.

"The look in your eyes when you recited it." He'd grown serious, was moving too close.

Tory increased her pace, wishing they'd reached her office already. "I can feel the love Longfellow felt for his daughters," she told him, and it was the simple truth. "I've been to his house, and I could almost sense his personality. 'From my study I see in the lamplight,/Descending the broad hall stair,/Grave Alice, and laughing Allegra,/And Edith with golden hair,'" she quoted. "I've stood in the study he was sitting in when he wrote that poem, looked up at the stairs—and on the wall are three portraits in descending order. Alice looks grave, pensive, Allegra is laughing, and Edith has beautiful golden hair." She paused, tried to describe the experience. "Being in a writer's house makes it so *real*. There's kind of an aura about a place like Longfellow's home, or Alcott's or Hawthorne's.''

''You make me want to go to New England. To tour all these places you've seen. To have this all come alive...and inspire me.''

''Isn't that what a teacher is supposed to do? Inspire her students?''

Except that she wasn't a teacher.

Or was she?

''History certainly comes to life when you're right there seeing it, touching it,'' she murmured. ''History and historical figures.''

''For some people,'' he said, moving aside as a young man sailed between them on a skateboard. ''I imagine there are a lot of people who tour those homes, see the same things you saw, and remain unimpressed.''

Feeling warm, though not from the October sun, Tory said, ''Maybe.''

''It's like those hats you told us about, the ones on Emerson's hat rack in his home. The way you described them, I could see the men who once owned them, sitting there discussing the state of the world. And it made Emerson's essays, his whole world, more real to me. Less abstract.''

She had no idea how he managed to see such good in her. And more amazing, to make her feel good about herself, during these few minutes she was with him.

Or was it Christine he made her feel good about?

''Phyllis and I had lunch with Becca Parsons on

Saturday,'' she said, slowing as they neared her building. She wanted her message delivered before they got there. She didn't want him to have any excuse to come inside with her.

"The president's wife, the one who did the biography on my great-grandfather.''

"That's right,'' Tory said, stopping outside the door of her office building. "She wants to meet you, Ben, to hear everything you're willing to tell her about your great-grandmother and the subsequent generations on that side of the family.''

He frowned. "I'm not sure I—''

"You don't have to tell her anything you don't want to,'' Tory assured him hastily. "Becca doesn't pry. You just find yourself talking to her. And she respects silence.'' Tory had found herself growing fond of the older woman as the three of them turned a one-hour lunch on Saturday into a three-hour discussion. They'd only left then because Becca had to get home to breastfeed her baby. Will jealously guarded his private time with his daughter, but there were some things he just couldn't do.

Shaking his head, Ben opened the door for her, then followed her inside and down the hall.

"She's eager to share what she knows about the Montfords with you, as well,'' Tory said.

She didn't know why getting Becca and Ben together had become so important to her. Her normal course was to stay out of other people's lives. Besides, she'd never been around long enough to play much of a part in them.

Except for Christine's, and look what a stellar job she'd done there.

For some reason, getting Ben to meet with Becca *mattered*. And she was afraid it mattered because she knew how much it would mean to him. He'd seemed starved for family connection that day he'd introduced her to his great-grandfather. Helping him find more of himself was a small thing she could do to thank him for the many times he'd unknowingly bolstered her these past weeks.

"I'll tell you what," he said as they reached Christine's office door. "I'll meet with her if you'll come along."

Tory stared at him. "Me?" she asked, pulling her keys out of the front pocket of her satchel. "Why should I be there?"

"Because I know you, and you know Becca Parsons."

And that was the only way he would agree to do this; Tory read it in his eyes. Despite her unease, she took only a moment to make her decision.

"Okay, I'll set up a time." She inserted her key into the lock. "What's good for you?"

"Any evening after five."

"I'll let you know...."

Tory turned to say goodbye to him before he could follow her into the office. She'd originally hoped to avoid even this much contact. Now she needed some space, some breathing room, a chance to get hold of herself. Fortunately, he was already heading down the hall.

"See ya," he called over his shoulder.

"Okay." Tory's relief was lost in the realization that Ben Sanders's butt looked darn good in snug blue jeans.

WEDNESDAY MORNING, Buddy peed on Ben's tennis shoe.

"Why'd you do that?" he asked the puppy none too nicely, as he held the little guy's neck so he could look him straight in the eye.

Buddy's tail drooped.

"You know better than this." Still holding the puppy's head, Ben swabbed up the mess with a paper towel. "Your papers are over there, the door's that way, and you know how to communicate. What do you think barking's for?"

Not fighting his captivity, Buddy watched. And listened. Or seemed to be listening.

"We've been over this before."

He'd thought the puppy was housebroken. Potty-training Alex had been easier.

Throwing his sneaker into a sinkful of soapy water, Ben slipped on a pair of brown leather tie-up shoes, the ones he usually reserved for wearing with Dockers, not with faded blue jeans. Then he grabbed his backpack and hurried out. The truck needed gas and he was now late.

The first station he went to had an electrical problem and the pumps were out of order.

Grumbling, he drove to the only other station in

town, just a block away, for pumps that worked. The gas was ten cents more per gallon.

There were no parking spots left in his usual lot when he finally got to school. He had to drive around to his second choice to find one. And getting out of the truck, he dropped his keys as he reached for the backpack he'd thrown on the seat earlier.

He bumped his head when he bent down to get the keys.

And swore a blue streak. Damn fine day this was turning out to be.

Christine had already started class by the time Ben got there. Embarrassed, he mouthed an apology from the doorway and hurried to his seat.

She was talking about James Fenimore Cooper, giving an overview of the man's life, the circumstances under which he wrote.

"Let's consider *The Last of the Mohicans*," she said. Ben pulled out the copy he'd reread over the weekend.

"On the surface, we have a heroic story, a savior…"

Ben nodded along with a few other people—probably the only other students who'd actually read the book. The rest were scribbling furiously, expecting to pass a test on a book they'd never read by taking notes in class.

"It's what made *The Last of the Mohicans* a classic, wouldn't you say?"

Everyone nodded.

She stood, as always, behind her desk, a barrier

between her and the class. She was wearing one of her prim-and-proper suits—navy today—and although Ben couldn't see her feet, he could guess which shoes she had on.

The woman was drop-dead gorgeous. Now that he'd seen her in street clothes, he realized that she knew how to dress, how to accentuate her beauty. So why in hell did she become so mousy in the classroom? She seemed to know her subject inside out, yet when she spoke about anything else, it was with a lack of confidence that amazed him.

"*The Last of the Mohicans* is a pop-culture epic written *by* a man *for* men," Christine said with more vehemence than he'd heard all semester.

It was the first time she'd been full of crap, too.

"Mark Twain had some pretty scathing things to say about Cooper's writing, but I didn't need his help to determine that *The Last of the Mohicans* is filled with shock tactics—or what would have been considered shock tactics at that time—plus gratuitous violence and a hero who's little more than an ego-bound male chauvinist posing as the good guy."

"I disagree." Ben hadn't meant to speak out loud. Hadn't realized he had until Christine's gaze pinned him to his seat. Every one of his twenty or more classmates was staring at him, too.

"Oh?" She raised an eyebrow.

"Hawkeye was a hero in every sense of the word. He fought for what was right, for what was true. He fought for the woman he loved, for her family and for the country.''

''He fought for his pride.''

She'd been so right about everything the entire semester. How could she be so far off course now?

''You'd rather a man not have any pride?'' he challenged, sliding down in his seat, his legs out in front of him. ''That's heroic?''

''This isn't about me.'' Christine crossed her arms over her chest—distracting him. ''We're talking about a man who wrote fantasy for other men. Cooper spoke of his times, tells *us* of his times, through story.''

''Hawkeye risked his life, repeatedly, for a battle that wasn't even his own,'' Ben said, although he told himself to keep his mouth shut. It wasn't even as if he cared all that much. He was just feeling ornery; it wasn't her fault he was having a bad day.

He might have shut up, too, in spite of all that, if he hadn't been so sure she was wrong.

If he hadn't spent another weekend thinking about her.

If he hadn't started thinking about the body beneath the clothes she wore—and the person inside that prim exterior.

''…which is why I agree with Ben,'' a girl a couple of rows over said. Ben had missed her argument, tuning in only for the last few words.

''But it's *why* he fought those battles that's the crux of the story,'' Christine said, not backing down an inch. ''He fought because he was proving something. He was a man proving to other men what real manhood was all about.''

"He fought because he cared," Ben said softly.

"Cared about what?"

Her gaze met and held his. Tapping his pen against his desk, Ben considered her question. Hawkeye cared about his woman, her sister and family. He cared about the wrongs being done to native Americans, cared about right and wrong.

But he also cared about his pride, about his own sense of manhood, about proving himself.

Ben might be completely right. And so might she.

He held his tongue.

"I SPOKE WITH Becca Parsons," Christine told Ben on Friday as he walked with her to her office on the way to his next class. He hadn't accompanied her after the previous English class, on Wednesday; he'd opted to head out to his truck, instead, and keep his disgruntled mood to himself. "She's invited us both to dinner next Friday night."

Dinner with Christine on Friday was really all Ben heard.

"Can you make it, or should I tell her another time would be better?"

Mentally checking his social calendar took about two seconds. "Next Friday's fine."

"You're sure you don't have other plans?" Christine asked, keeping her usual distance from him.

"I shoot hoops with Zack Foster now and then, when he can get away. Which isn't often, because his partner, Cassie Tate, is out of town a lot with her pet-therapy project,'' Ben said. ''I walk my dog every day. That's the extent of my social life.''

''Oh.''

''How about you? Don't you have something planned for a Friday night?''

She grinned at him, almost as though for a moment there, she'd forgotten she was his teacher and he her student. ''I water Phyllis's plants, occasionally do things with her and some of her friends. That's the extent of *my* social life.''

Hands in the pockets of his jeans, Ben grinned back at her.

''Becca and Will have a new baby,'' Christine said, looking straight ahead again, her brows drawn together in a slight frown he was beginning to recognize all too well. No one could worry as much as this woman appeared to.

''You sound as though that's a warning,'' Ben said, enjoying the balmy late-October seventy-degree weather.

Christine shrugged. ''A lot of people aren't comfortable around children.''

Guess it depended on what kind of people you associated with.

''I love kids,'' Ben told her. ''How old is their baby?''

''Not quite two months.''

With a pang, Ben remembered Alex at that age. She'd been following him with her eyes by then, able to focus and recognize him. She'd smiled some, too, though Mary had insisted it was only gas. Ben knew better.

"I remember those days well," he murmured. He'd barely been eighteen when Alex was born, but he'd been so crazy about her that fatherhood hadn't daunted him a bit. Supporting Alex's mother—and putting up with her—had done that.

"Those days?"

They'd reached Christine's building.

"I told you I'd married young," Ben said, reaching for the door to the building.

Nodding, Christine stopped just outside.

"It was because my wife was pregnant."

Her jaw dropped as she stared at him. "You have a child?"

"That's so hard to believe?" Ben motioned her through the door, following her inside.

"Yes! Well—" she turned, looked at him again "—no, I guess not, but you never said anything."

He shrugged. "What was there to say? I loved. I lost. End of story."

Her office door was straight ahead. Christine fished her key out of her leather satchel, unlocked the door.

"I just can't picture you as a father."

Ben walked into her office and half closed the door, just enough to ensure privacy. In deference to her skittishness, he had to leave it partially open.

"I was a damn good father," he said, his voice calm and clear. There was to be no misunderstanding that. Raising Alex was the one thing he'd done right in the past seven years, the only thing that made the passage of those years palatable.

"Was? You aren't anymore?" Christine stood behind her desk, but the warmth in her eyes reached out to him.

"Nope." He toyed with the rock that served as a paperweight on her desk.

She sank into her chair. "What happened?" she whispered. "Did the baby die?"

He hadn't intended to have this conversation. Ben perched stiffly on the other chair. "The baby was a girl and no, she didn't die. She's living in California with her mother and new father."

"You don't visit her at all? Even out-of-state fathers get a weekend a month, or the summer and some holidays."

"I'm not her father."

CHAPTER EIGHT

"EXCUSE ME?"

Christine frowned, although the warmth was still very apparent in her eyes, very apparent in its effect on him.

"Mary, my ex-wife, told me the child was mine." He shrugged, looked away from her. "We'd been... together only a few times." His gaze found hers again. "But I believed her."

"How long did you support her before you found out you were off the hook?"

She'd changed on him again, become the woman who didn't believe—not in a father's love, not in heroism, not in much of anything, it seemed. What got to him most, though, was that she didn't sound bitter or hard. Her voice was as soft, as understanding as it had been since the whole crazy conversation began.

"I'll never be off the hook," Ben told her honestly.

"You're still supporting her?"

No. But he would if Mary let him. He'd do anything to be part of Alex's life. "I'm still loving her."

Christine's held tilted, the slight frown in evidence once more. "Oh."

"I raised Alex." Ben couldn't stop, now that he'd started. Couldn't stop until Christine understood how it was with him. "From the moment she was born, she was my responsibility."

"Her mother didn't want her." It wasn't a question, merely acceptance of a fact. A fact that seemed all too ordinary, which startled him a little.

"No, although I didn't realize that until after we were married." Mary had kept all the surprises until she had him where she wanted him. Then, over the next seven or so years, they just kept coming.

Until the last little bombshell she'd dropped.

"Alex and I were a team," Ben said, smiling as he remembered. "When I was working at the garage, I'd take her with me. She'd trail along behind me whenever she could, asking a million questions."

"You said you worked two jobs. Surely you didn't keep a young child out late at night."

"No." He shook his head, crossed a leg over his knee, tapped his hand on his shin. "Mary was home with her then, at least some of the time. Al went to bed early, so there wasn't a lot required of Mary. As Alex got older, I hired a baby-sitter."

"Where was your wife?"

"Out. With friends." He'd stopped asking years ago.

Christine took a deep breath, let it out slowly. She leaned forward, elbows on her desk, resting her chin in her palms. She looked relaxed, caring. Beautiful. "So what happened?"

"About a year ago, I came home from work one day to find my wife with another man."

"In your house?" She didn't seem at all shocked by the sordid tale.

"That month's apartment, you mean?" Ben asked. And then added, "In our bed."

"I'm sorry."

"It happens," Ben said, throwing his hands wide before letting them fall back on his leg. "That wasn't the worst of it. The real kicker was when she introduced him to me."

Face pale, Christine sat up. "Alex's father," she said breathlessly.

Hanging on to the compassion in her eyes, Ben nodded. "He and Mary had been lovers since she was fifteen. He'd been sent up to prison for car theft, among other things, just before she met me. When she found out she was pregnant, I was convenient."

"The bitch."

Ben shrugged again. "I got Alex out of it."

"I can't believe she did that!"

Finally something had shocked her. After everything he'd told her without garnering much reaction, Ben was a bit surprised.

"Seems she was visiting ol' Pete in jail the entire time I was working my butt off to support her," Ben said. Might as well tell her the rest. Let her know what a total sap he'd been.

Ben the fool. The one who always cleaned up other people's messes. Ben the doormat.

"I'm sorry." This time the words were accompanied by a sheen of tears in her eyes.

"Yeah, well, even that didn't faze me much at that point. What got me was when they told me just how expendable I was. I wasn't needed anymore. Pete was free, had a job. Mary wanted a divorce. Pete was going to step in and be an instant father to the child he'd never seen."

"And the courts allowed it because he was her natural father."

He nodded. "There was no point in contesting the divorce, but I hadn't realized when it happened that Mary would be awarded full custody."

"Wasn't there something you could do? Some way to fight the decision?"

He had fought. And lost. Besides, something the social worker had said had hit him very hard. "If I loved Alex, wouldn't I want her to have this chance?"

"Is he good to her?" Christine asked, her eyes narrowed. "Does he love her?"

He didn't know. Couldn't stomach the fact that Pete might not adore Alex. Prayed every night that he did. "Not as much as I do," Ben said. And then, "I'm sure he must love her. He fought for his right to be her father."

"You don't have any contact with her at all?"

He lifted a hand. "The courts advised that it would be best for Alex if Mary and Pete allowed her and me to stay in touch. However, Mary decided it wasn't fair to Pete to have me in the picture. She said Alex wasn't giving Pete a chance.''

"What do you think?''

"I only want what's best for Alex.'' He just wasn't sure what that was. His gut was telling him one thing, his head another. His gut said Alex needed him. His mind said maybe there was some truth in what Mary said, that Alex's love for him, loyalty to him, interfered with her ability to give her heart to her real father.

With both elbows still on her desk, Christine folded her hands in front of her. "What does Alex want?''

"She wants me to go live in the spare room in their house.'' She hadn't asked him to take her away from Pete, he reminded himself. Just to be a part of their family.

"We stay in touch, in spite of Mary.'' Ben needed to assure Christine—and to hear the words himself. "I taught Alex how to call me collect.''

"And does she?''

"Once, so far.''

"Was she all right?''

"That's the hell of it,'' he said. "I'm not sure.''

"Did she sound happy?''

"Not any kind of happy I ever heard from her before.'' Ben told Christine about Alex's odd question, about the child's urgency. And about being left alone at night.

"If they were just across the street, they could probably see the house."

"And would they have been able to see into the bathroom if Alex woke up sick to her stomach? Or hear her crying if she had a bad dream and was frightened?"

Christine gave him a compassionate smile. "And how often do you think either of those things are going to happen?"

"I don't know," Ben admitted. "But they could, and as her parents they should be there, just in case."

He damn sure would have been.

"In a perfect world, maybe."

Yeah. In a perfect world. Ben could tell by the look in her eyes that Christine didn't believe, for one second, that a perfect world existed. Anywhere.

He still believed.

LATE FRIDAY AFTERNOON, Tory had an English Department faculty meeting, where she sat silently as usual, taking notes and nodding her head. She knew a lot about American literature, was spending every spare moment educating herself on the material she taught, but she knew next to nothing about pedagogy or administration. And with all the time she was spending on class preparation, she wasn't able to read education texts as well.

Right now, she had an excuse for her silence. She was new to Montford, was only learning about the procedures under which the college operated. She'd lucked out in that regard, because most colleges had their own brand of administrative claptrap. There wasn't some universal set of rules she was expected to know.

She left immediately after the meeting so she didn't have to walk out to the parking lot by herself, and then, waving goodbye to Christine's colleagues, people she barely knew, people who intimidated her, she locked herself in her car, a free woman for two whole days.

Always on the alert, Tory noticed a car appear behind her, almost from nowhere, as she pulled out onto the main thoroughfare through town. It was a sedan again. But not, she thought with relief, the same sedan. This one was a light tan color. Of course, turning in one rental car for another to throw her off track was no big feat.

Any staff Bruce's family kept on retainer, whether caterers, gardeners or detectives, were good. And after more than two years of tailing her, the investigators knew *she* was good. They'd taught her well. She'd also taught them. She'd be on to them in a second if she noticed the same car hanging around.

She took the next corner. So did the sedan.

Heart beating fast, cold with the dread of another lost hope, another lost life, Tory thought about speeding out of town, losing whoever was behind her on desert roads…and then losing herself out there, too.

The light at the corner of Main and Montford turned red. The tan sedan was two cars back. Right or left, she wondered. Tucson or Phoenix? Or should she just go north—toward Canada?

She'd never been to Canada. Europe a couple of times with Bruce, early in their marriage. Hong Kong. The Greek Islands. Mexico. But never Canada.

Main was bustling as Shelter Valley residents celebrated the advent of the weekend, cashed Friday's paychecks, shopped. Kids were everywhere, talking with friends on the corner, eating ice cream outside the drugstore, buying Halloween costumes at Weber's. College students were in abundance, too, though Tory suspected that a lot of them were heading into Phoenix for the evening.

With the light green, Tory slid into an empty parking slot on the other side of Main. She jumped out and made her way nonchalantly into Weber's, where she'd have a view of the street from the big front window. And where she was safest. Anyone with dangerous motives would have real trouble getting past the residents of this town.

She didn't really belong here, and yet, in a sense, she did. People recognized her now, smiled at her when she met them at the diner with Phyllis or passed them on the street downtown. She'd been hired at Montford U. That made her one of them.

And Shelter Valley protected its own.

The tan car drove right past Weber's.

Tory, grabbing some panty hose and a new slip, walked casually to the cash register. She knew the sense of relief washing over her was deceptive. Just because the car passed—this time—didn't mean it hadn't been following her.

"How're you doing today Dr….Evans, isn't it?" Mr. Weber asked as he rang up her purchases.

"It is," Tory said, "and I'm fine. Looking forward to the weekend."

Mr. Weber nodded. He wasn't much older than Will Parsons, and in equally good shape. "My wife and I are having our son and daughter-in-law down from Phoenix…."

He continued to tell her about his plans while he took her money—Tory always used cash—and bagged her purchases. Tory continued to listen.

By the time she made it back to her car, she was feeling much more in control. There was always a chance the car *hadn't* been following her, she supposed.

Given the events of the past couple of years, she was bound to have developed some phobias. An unfounded fear of being followed could certainly be one of them.

THE WEEKEND PASSED far too swiftly. Tory went into Phoenix with Phyllis and Martha Moore to catch a movie on Saturday night. She loved the new theater they took her to, with high-backed seats on raised levels that made her feel completely hidden from those behind her. They saw an adult comedy that was entertaining enough to have all three of them laughing out loud. She appreciated the conversation before and after the movie, too.

Going through a divorce after more than twenty years of marriage, Martha was grappling with some serious issues regarding her own personal worth— and strength. Tory's heart went out to her.

Tory was home alone on Friday afternoon of the following week, the radio playing in the background, as she thought about Martha, folded a load of laundry and tried not to think about the evening ahead. Phyllis, at Tory's pleading, had been going to accompany her and Ben to the Parsons home for Ben's meeting with Becca, but then Martha had called, needing to be two places at once with her kids, and Phyllis had offered to pinch-hit for her.

A shirt of Christine's, one of Tory's favorites, was still warm from the dryer as Tory buttoned it on its hanger. Holding it up to her face, she tried not to give in to the despair that threatened. She blinked back tears, as she often did when donning her older sister's clothes, clothes she'd decided to keep and wear, when she was playing Christine. It helped her remember who she was. And who she wasn't.

Undies, bras, pajamas, were all neatly folded and ready to put in drawers. Dressed in a pair of sweatpants and an old T-shirt, Tory worked methodically. Radio ads—a Phoenix car dealer having a sale, the benefits of laser eye surgery, a furniture sale—accompanied her while she worked. Open a drawer. Close a drawer. Routine. Comforting. No stress.

She was glad to be alone, finding occasions like this the only times she could ever be just plain old Tory Evans, whoever that was. She didn't have to watch her thoughts or her back, didn't have to worry about how her problems or her mood were affecting anyone else.

A Bette Midler song came on—the song about one person being another's hero.

Panties slid from her fingers and fell onto her bare toes.

Oh, God.

As though in a trance, Tory sank onto the bed, drawn into the song.

Yeah, she might have attempted to fly away, like the lyrics said, but only because she'd had Christine there, giving her impetus.

She shuddered, her body suffused with heat, and then shivering. How many hundreds of times had she sung along with Bette Midler, thinking of her older sister? The song, every single word of it, could have been written for her and Christine.

Tears seeped through her lashes as Tory listened. She had no choice. The song was speaking to her.

Had Christine been cold and lonely, always in the background, emotionally supporting Tory, protecting her?

While Christine had stayed home and worked, studied, made something of herself, Tory had been flying off to Europe with Bruce, jet-setting with the rich and famous. Her life had swung between violence and frivolity. Christine had given her the strength to break free.

"Christine, how am I ever going to make it?" she

cried as the song finally ended. "And why should I even try?"

"Because you're alive." The words fell softly into the room, and Tory glanced up to see Phyllis standing there, still in the navy dress she'd worn to work, her eyes filled with sympathy—and pain.

"I didn't hear you come in," Tory said. "I thought you were going straight to the football game." Phyllis had agreed to run the concession at Martha's son's game.

Sitting down beside her on the bed, Phyllis rubbed Tory's back. "I got out of my meeting early," she said quietly. "And I'm glad I did. Is this what you do with yourself when I'm gone?"

"Not usually." Tory gave her a watery grin. "It was just that song." She teared up again. "It always made me think of her, but...but I never told her that."

"I'll bet she knows."

"You think so?"

"I know so."

Tory wanted to believe Phyllis, to believe that somehow her sister was an angel watching down on her from heaven. Wanted to believe in *something*.

"You okay to go tonight?" Phyllis asked. The red hair framing her face appeared almost like a halo to Tory.

Shaking her head at her little-girl fantasy, Tory straightened. Ben would be by to get her in less than an hour. "Yeah, I just have to change."

"And redo your makeup."

Glancing at her mascara-streaked face in the mirror, Tory smiled. "That, too." She bent to pick up the panties she'd dropped.

Phyllis stood, lifting the empty laundry basket. "You sure you're okay about riding out there with him?"

"Yeah." Oddly enough, although she felt a little nervous about being alone with a man—any man—in a vehicle he was driving, the thought of riding with Ben Sanders wasn't sending her into a panic attack.

Stopping in the doorway, basket on her hip, Phyllis turned back to her. "Maybe you should wear those black stretchy slacks that look like you've been poured into them." She paused. "And the white ribbed top."

Also tight. Tory shook her head. "I'm not out to spark the man's interest, Phyllis."

"Why not?"

"I don't know." Tory stared down her friend. "Maybe because I'm living a lie?"

"Maybe," Phyllis agreed, "and if I thought that was the only thing holding you back, I might let you off the hook. But it isn't, is it? You've met a nice man, one who interests *you,* and you're scared to death of that."

"Like I said—because I'm living a lie."

Phyllis shook her head. "Because you're afraid to believe that good people really exist."

"They don't. Not in my world."

"Then what am I?" Phyllis's gaze wouldn't let Tory escape.

"You're the best friend anyone could ever hope to have," Tory whispered. "Christine was very lucky to find you."

"You found me, too, Tory," Phyllis said gently. "And someday, you're going to believe that."

She was gone before Tory could reply.

CHAPTER NINE

"I LIKE YOUR TRUCK," Tory told Ben an hour later as they drove slowly up the winding road that led to Becca and Will's home halfway up the mountain overlooking Shelter Valley.

"Thanks."

"I've always wanted a truck," Tory said wistfully.

"So why'd you buy a Mustang?"

"It was easy to maneuver, fast—" Tory stopped. The words made her sound like a kid. Ben couldn't know that she had to have a vehicle that could slide out of tough spots on a second's notice.

Ben glanced her way and then quickly back to the road. "You look nice."

She'd worn the black pants. Just to show Phyllis she wasn't afraid.

But she was.

"Thanks."

He looked good, too. He was wearing brown slacks with a tan corduroy shirt that rippled across the shoulders every time he turned the steering wheel. His curly dark hair, just touching the edge of his collar, looked soft and clean—something a woman might want to run her fingers through.

Not Tory, of course, but a woman who was free and whole and able to love.

AT THE HEAD of his dining-room table, Will leaned back in his chair, replete. As usual, Becca's ham-and-apricot casserole had been superb. He was enjoying their company. And, in another half hour or so, Bethany would be awake for her eight-o'clock feeding. Life didn't get much better than this.

"Did you grow up on the reservation?" Becca, resting her arms on the table, asked their guest. She'd been keeping him occupied with one question after another from the moment they'd sat down to dinner.

"Maybe the man would like to catch his breath, Bec," Will told her, loving the excited glow in her eyes even as he took pity on Ben Sanders.

She nodded. "I'm sorry, Ben. Am I making you uncomfortable?" she asked.

"No." Ben's gaze slid to Christine and then back to Becca. "It's hard to be offended when you care so much about the ancestors I've been waiting most of my life to find."

"So *did* you grow up on the reservation?" Christine asked.

She'd been quiet most of the evening, but that was how Will remembered her from the interview last spring. A quiet woman with sad eyes. There was something changed about her, though. She seemed less confident somehow. Remembering how difficult it had been for Becca and her sister Sari to deal with Sari's daughter's death a few years before, Will figured Christine must be experiencing something similar. Her own sister's death was still recent, and as sudden and unexpected as his niece's death had been.

Christine looked different, too. Had lost a lot of weight over the summer, cut her hair much shorter.

"No, I didn't grow up on the reservation," Ben was answering quietly. The young man was mature beyond his years. As though he'd already learned a whole life's worth of lessons.

"My father was born there, lived there until he was sixteen. His father, John Cloud, had been killed in a hunting accident when he was still a young boy, and his mother, Samuel Montford's daughter, died when he was about ten. Gradually my grandfather's people became less tolerant of the half-breed kid who preferred to wear his hair short and wasn't particularly interested in Indian ways. They'd loved my grandmother dearly, had accepted her as one of them and, out of respect for her, I guess, had put up with her son, as well, but after she was gone..."

Ben's voice drifted off as he shrugged and took a sip from the cup of coffee Becca had placed before him.

"It was just as Samuel Montford had feared," Christine said. Will was rather surprised to see this private and subdued young woman so enthralled by the story. Pleasantly surprised. "Some people still seem to have a hard time accepting racially mixed unions," she elaborated.

"Especially if there are children," Becca added.

"I guess." Ben ran his finger along the edge of his saucer, frowned. "He also had a hard time finding his place in the white man's world."

"A man without a people," Will said, feeling himself supremely blessed. He knew who he was, who his people were, past and present.

"He changed his name and married my mother, a white woman, and had me—but it only lasted about ten years," Ben continued. "I don't know if you're aware of it, but physiologically, many Indians don't have a high tolerance for alcohol. Something about a missing enzyme—"

"Which is why most reservations in this state are dry," Becca interjected.

"They are?" Christine's brows rose.

Will nodded. "There are some places in Phoenix—businesses, including casinos—that are built on rented Indian land, and because of that, can't get a liquor license."

"My father inherited that low tolerance from his father," Ben said.

Will felt for the younger man, knowing what was coming next.

"He started drinking when he moved off the reservation," Becca guessed, mirroring, as she often did, Will's thoughts.

Ben brushed crumbs into a pile on the tablecloth. "He couldn't hold onto a job, or a home, either. And every time we had to move, it was the fault of whatever town we were in, whatever people we dealt with. Everyone was prejudiced against him because he was a half-breed.''

''I'm sure there was some truth in that,'' Will said.

Becca smiled at him. ''Will's had to do battle for a number of Indian students over the years. The injustice this country has handed out to its aboriginal people is something that can always be counted on to raise his blood pressure.''

Maybe. But nothing could raise his blood pressure like she could. In the most thrilling way....

''There *was* some truth to it,'' Ben said, ''but it was also an excuse, a resentment he carried with him to his grave.''

Frowning, Christine pushed her coffee cup away. ''Did you have brothers and sisters?''

''Nope. I think by the time I was born, my mother was already disillusioned and that I'm the reason she hung on as long as she did. She took me with her when she finally left him, but died the next year— complications from diabetes. I was sent back to Dad....''

Will jumped up as his ready ears picked up the faint sound from the bassinet in the other room.

''The baby's awake,'' Ben said, standing, too. He followed Will out of the room.

''Come here, sweet girl,'' Will crooned to his infant daughter, lifting her out of her bassinet for a hug and a couple of kisses before laying her back down.

Ben watched him change the baby's diaper. "You do that a lot," he said.

"You sound as though you know what you're talking about, too."

"My daughter was born when I was eighteen," Ben said. "Used to do a lot of the caring for her myself."

Will turned, his hand spanning the baby's stomach as he looked at Ben. "Used to?"

"Turns out she wasn't mine biologically. She's living with her mother and real father as of this summer."

"That's rough," Will commiserated. He couldn't imagine anything more awful than losing Bethany. Except losing Becca.

He'd come close to doing that earlier in the year and knew firsthand that it was an experience worse than death. To be dead while still alive...

"Mind if I hold her?" Ben asked as Will finished changing Bethany.

"No, of course not."

Watching, Will was impressed with the way Ben gently held Bethany, cradling her head protectively. But it was the genuine look of delight on the man's face that won Will over completely.

Ben Sanders was quite a guy.

A woman would be lucky to have him on her side.

And his new professor looked as though she needed a little luck.

Unfortunately Ben Sanders was off-limits to her because he was her student—at least for the current semester.

Christine glanced up when Will and Ben walked back into the room, her eyes darting to the baby in Ben's arms and then away.

"You want to hold her?" Ben asked. "She's not fussing yet."

"You've got about five minutes." Becca laughed. "If she's not eating by then, she'll scream the house down."

"No—you go ahead," Christine answered Ben, smiling awkwardly.

Will was relieved to see that awkwardness. When Becca had told him the two of them would be arriving together, he'd gotten the same sick feeling he'd had last spring when he'd heard rumors about Todd Moore's possible liaison with a student.

He'd had to force his best friend, who was also head of Montford's Psychology department, to resign when the rumors turned out to be true.

He sure as hell didn't want to see the same thing happening to Christine Evans. He barely knew the woman, but he'd had a soft spot for her from the first time they'd met.

Maybe Becca could suggest someone for Christine. That might be the best solution. Invite them both to their annual Christmas party—if they had one.

With Bethany in the house, he didn't dare plan too far ahead. He never knew what she'd dictate from one minute to the next and had already changed his plans so many times in the weeks since she was born that he knew better than to be sure of anything.

But he was damn glad to have her dictating. Thankful for the sometimes sleepless nights, the curtailed freedom, the smelly diapers and stained shirts.

And would be thankful until his dying day that Becca was there, sharing the whole experience with him.

He'd almost lost her. He was never going to forget that or how fortunate he was to have this second chance. The first twenty years he'd lived with Becca, he'd taken their love for granted. He planned to spend the next fifty years fully aware of its value.

As Christine walked out to Ben's truck a short while later, he couldn't help but hope that someday his wife might able to work a little magic on her, too.

"SO TELL ME about your family," Ben said, steering his truck slowly down the winding mountain road that served as the Parsonses' drive. Christine sat stiffly beside him, staring straight ahead. He didn't know if it was his probing that was making her uncomfortable or the steep dark road.

"Why?"

He shrugged. "Seems only fair, considering that you've just heard every intimate detail of three generations of mine."

"There's not much to tell."

"It's safe to assume that at one point in your life you had parents." Something made him persist. Desert brush loomed in front of them, shadowy and large.

Christine nodded, her face, when he stole a quick glance, expressionless. No warm memories there.

"Are they still alive?"

She shook her head. And then nothing. Were the wounds still that raw? Or so old they didn't matter?

"I'm sorry," he said, slowing the truck further as the shadows grew closer to the road.

"Don't be."

"They've been gone a long time, then?"

"My mother died when I was ten."

His heart lurched. "That must have been hard."

Silence.

"What about your father?"

"I never knew him."

Reaching the end of the mountain drive, Ben turned the truck toward town. He wasn't in any hurry to drop her off.

"Then who raised you after your mother died?"

"My sister."

"She was that much older than you?" Ben asked, glancing sideways. Her features were still. "Old enough to have custody of a ten-year-old?"

"Our stepfather lived with us."

There was really nothing different in the way she'd said the words, no change in the monotone she'd been using since the conversation began, and yet, Ben felt a new chill.

"Is he still around?" he asked cautiously.

"He died of lung cancer a couple of years ago."

Ben had lost both of his parents, as well. But she already knew that. A car approached them, its headlights momentarily blinding.

"When you're little you think your parents are going to live forever," he mused, "or at least long enough to get old and be grandparents…"

He paused, slowed to turn. Christine remained silent beside him, her gaze on the road.

"Makes it even harder to lose them when it happens long before it's time."

"Yeah," she said so softly he barely heard her, "it does."

He heard the pain in her voice, felt it with her.

"What about your sister?" he asked, hoping to ease that pain a bit. "Was it just the two of you, or did you have other siblings?"

"It was just the two of us."

"Where is she now? Still back East?" Ben wanted to meet her, to unravel at least part of the mystery that was Christine.

"She's buried in New Mexico."

Oh, God.

"What happened?"

"A car accident." The words were staccato, suspended by the pain that accompanied them.

He'd reached the turnoff for her street, but pulled into the gravel lot at the park, instead, stopping the car beneath a tree. Only the moon's reflection illuminated them, a confusing contrast of light and shadow.

"You want to talk about it?" he asked as Christine sat unmoving beside him. She hadn't even acknowledged that he'd stopped the truck.

"There's nothing to tell. The car went off the road. She was killed."

Had it not been for the raw anguish he glimpsed briefly in her eyes, Ben might have been able to let it go at that.

"How long ago?" he asked.

"Not quite two months."

He turned to face her. "Just before classes started?" It explained so much. Her stoicism, her unusual reticence. Christine was in the throes of grief.

Throes he knew only too well.

Perhaps this also explained why he'd felt such an unusual connection to her.

"What was her name?" Would it help her to talk about it?

"T-tory," she said, still not looking at him. He had a feeling she wasn't seeing the grassy area and park benches in front of them, either.

Compelled by something stronger than his own reason, Ben brushed one hand across her cheek, undaunted when she flinched. With a soothing motion he remembered from his own childhood, he smoothed her bangs away from her face.

"Don't!" she cried, pulling back sharply.

But not before his hand had felt the uneven ridge of skin on her forehead.

He brushed her bangs again, holding them up so

he could see her forehead in the moonlight. No longer fighting him, Christine closed her eyes.

The scar was angry-looking, long, puffy, as though the tear had been too ragged to repair neatly. And still pink. It was recent.

"You were in the car, too." His heart in his throat, he knew he was right.

Christine nodded. Tears crept out from beneath her lowered eyelids to slide down her cheek.

"Were you driving?"

She shook her head. And then nodded. Ben figured it didn't much matter one way or the other. Except...

Christine seemed so unhappy with herself, so lacking in confidence, in self-love. Could this be why?

"Was it your fault?" he asked, knowing that regardless what had happened, the accident was simply that, an accident.

Christine nodded. Another tear escaped. The woman was consumed by grief and guilt, and Ben couldn't leave it like that.

"Tell me about it."

"Th-there's not much to tell," she said, her voice shaky. She turned her head away, looked out the passenger window. "A-another car came around the curve when we did. We swerved too close to the edge and went over."

"Was he passing you?"

"I guess."

"And you were in your lane?"

"Yeah."

"Sounds to me like the other car was at fault."

She shrugged, still facing away from him.

"Were you cited?"

She shook her head. "No one was. They considered it a one-car accident and didn't charge me."

He longed to pull her into his arms, to place her head on his chest and shoulder the burdens that were too heavy for her to bear alone. He ran his fingers through the ends of her hair, then lightly stroked her shoulder and the back of her neck.

Her muscles were tight, strained. He continued to massage gently, but she didn't melt into his touch, didn't relax at all. She didn't pull away, either.

"If the law doesn't blame you, why do you blame yourself?" he asked after a while.

She was silent for so long he didn't think she was going to answer him. Despite that, he was ready to sit there as many hours as she'd allow him to offer whatever comfort he could, even if that was only by barely touching her neck.

"We were on our way to Arizona." It was an effort to make out the words. "She wouldn't have been coming out here if not for me."

He could tell her that didn't make the accident her fault. He could insist that the decision to accompany her had been Tory's, that neither one of them was to blame if the fates had chosen that particular moment to send a reckless driver across their path. He could have told her—but he didn't. It would have done nothing to help her.

"The night my father died, he'd been drinking," Ben said, instead, taking comfort himself now from the brief physical contact. "And the more he drank, the more bitter he got, until this commercial came on about an Indian and littering. The one where someone driving by on the highway throws a bag of trash at an Indian's feet. I don't know if my father was feeling his Indian heritage at that moment or his own bitterness, but he threw his glass at the television set.'' Ben could still see the shards flying. ''The glass shattered and the whiskey dripped down the screen.''

Christine didn't move, her head still turned away. But her breathing was growing heavier. She was listening.

''It was nothing he hadn't done before, in some way or other. I just happened to have a friend over that night.''

Her muscles lurched beneath his fingers.

''Then Dad decided he was going to the bar, and instead of stopping him like I usually did, I let him go. I was so damned humiliated, so eager to have him gone, I practically started the car for him.''

He paused, concentrated on the warmth of her skin underneath her blouse, the fragile bones at the base of her neck.

''He never made it to the bar—and I never saw him again.''

Turning to face him, Christine met his gaze, her eyes filled with more warmth than he'd ever seen.

''He wrapped his car around a tree,'' Ben said in a whisper.

CHAPTER TEN

"SURELY YOU DON'T blame yourself for your father's death?" Tory asked, able to breathe again, to speak, now that she was no longer the topic of conversation.

"On occasion," he admitted.

Tory found it nearly impossible to have compassion for a man. But she hated to think of Ben torturing himself when it wasn't necessary. She knew about alcoholics. Had spent most of her life at the mercy of two of them.

"It was his drinking that killed him," she said, speaking in the authoritative voice she'd learned to use in her classroom. The voice that said she knew what she was talking about.

In this case, she did.

"The fact remains, if I'd kept him home as I usually did..."

"Then he might have lived through that night," Tory allowed. "But you couldn't be with him every night for the rest of his life, Ben. There was bound to be a time when he was going to drink and drive."

The muscles in his jaw were working. Tory

wished she dared look into his eyes, to see what he was thinking.

"And if it'd been a later time, a different time, there might have been other people involved in his accident, as well. He might have killed innocent people, along with himself."

Besides, why blame yourself when a rotten man dies? Tory asked silently. *No need for blame when the world is done a favor.*

"You can't be responsible for another man's choices," she said.

He shifted to look at her, his hand on the back of her neck. "Neither can you."

Bowing her head, Tory leaned forward, away from his touch. His hand was too heavy suddenly, a weight she couldn't hold.

"I know," she said, because she had to. Any other response would raise more questions. Questions she wasn't willing to answer.

But Tory knew she couldn't escape the guilt so easily. Because she *was* to blame. Christine was dead because of decisions Tory had made. It was that simple, that inescapable—from the day she married Bruce to the day she agreed to come west with Christine. She'd convinced herself to believe that she'd be safe because she'd wanted it so badly. But she'd known Bruce would find her. He always did.

Christine was the one who'd made all the right decisions. She'd *died* making a right decision. She'd chosen to be honorable and true and to take care of her baby sister, as she'd promised their dying mother. Christine was the Evans girl with a future, with a reason for living, the Evans girl worthy of life.

Other than loving her sister, Tory hadn't done much of anything worthy in her life. She hadn't done much of anything, period.

Except run.

"I'VE LOST EIGHT POUNDS!" Phyllis announced the next morning.

Looking up from the Robert Frost anthology she was studying, Tory smiled at Phyllis.

"I'm proud of you!" Her friend was wearing a pair of Guess jeans that were no longer tight at the waist. "And you didn't have to starve yourself."

Parading around the living room in front of Tory, Phyllis grinned. "Who'd have thought just leaving that last bite on my plate would make such a difference?"

"The one bite by itself probably doesn't, but leaving it there makes a statement," Tory said, pulling her legs up beside her on the couch. She was wearing sweatpants and a T-shirt, but she'd forgotten her socks, and her feet were cold. "That last bite says you're done, and it's proof that you believe it, and you don't eat anymore."

"Is that how you've always stayed so slim?"

Tory shrugged. The game was something her mother had invented. One of the few memories she had of the woman she'd adored.

Tory had never needed it, though. Life curtailed her appetite.

"I've still got a long way to go...."

"And you'll get there," Tory said with certainty. Phyllis was one of those women with unending strength. She'd do whatever she set her mind to.

"What do you mean?" Phyllis asked, frowning. "You're still with me on this, aren't you? You'll still coach me?"

"Of course." As long as Phyllis thought she needed her.

"Okay." Phyllis glanced down at the book on Tory's lap. "After you finish learning far more about next week's class than any teacher needs to know, you want to hit some of those exclusive shops in Scottsdale and get me some new clothes?"

"Sure!" Tory might even splurge and buy something for herself.

Phyllis sat on the other end of the couch. "So how was your date last night?"

Frost's *The Freedom of the Moon* suddenly filled Tory's vision. "It wasn't a date." She stared fiercely at the page.

It wasn't her favorite poem, either. So much ethereal beauty it hurt. She flipped through the book, knowing she'd have to come back. She had to teach an overview of Frost. She couldn't just include the poems she liked.

"Call it what you want," Phyllis said, her elbow resting on the arm of the couch. "Did you have a good time with Ben?"

"I wasn't with Ben. I was with Becca and Will, and yes, dinner was very nice. Becca's a good cook." And Will wasn't quite as intimidating when he was gushing all over his baby daughter.

"Was Bethany awake?"

Tory nodded. She'd found the poem she wanted. "The Road Not Taken." The one about two roads diverging.

"Did you hold her?"

She'd been afraid to. Afraid that tiny innocent and defenseless body would make her cry. Or that she'd make the baby cry. "There was only a minute or two before Becca had to feed her, and Ben got to her first."

"He held the baby?"

Yet knowing how way leads on to way,/I doubted if I should ever come back, Tory read silently.

The sight of that baby held so tenderly in those big arms had almost made her cry, too. "He just picked her up and started crooning to her," she told Phyllis, looking up from the book for a second.

Phyllis slid down and swung her feet onto the couch. "Ben seems special. He's kind—look how he humored Becca, giving up a Friday night to share his family history. Considerate. Gentle—handling a baby that way. And gorgeous, too!"

Tory knew where this was going—and where it couldn't go. "He's my student."

"He's as old as you are."

"Did you read your Montford-faculty manual?" Tory asked, studying the poem again. "Teachers are expressly forbidden to fraternize with their students.''

"They're forbidden to have sexual relations with them," Phyllis specified, making Tory even more uncomfortable. "And correct me if I'm off the mark, but your having sex isn't something we need to be worrying about anytime soon."

"He's my student." Tory barely got the words past the constriction in her throat.

"Only for another six weeks. The rules only apply when he's in your class, not when he's in someone else's. Besides, you and I both know that in your case, the rules don't really apply at all."

Tory went back to her roads. She'd definitely taken the one less traveled.

And that made all the difference.

"...COLLECT CALL. Will you accept the charges?''

"Yes, of course." Bolting upright in bed, Ben wiped the sleep from his eyes, coming fully awake with the phone in his hand. He barely remembered answering it.

"Daddy?"

"Alex? What's the matter?" he asked, trying to keep his voice soft and calm. His baby girl was crying. And Alex wasn't a crier.

"We were wrong, Daddy," Alex said, and then ruined her attempt to sound brave with a hiccup.

Ben glanced at the clock—and then looked again. It was one o'clock in the morning. A Tuesday morning.

"What did we do wrong, Al?" What was she doing up at this hour? And where in hell was Mary that Alex was able to get to a phone to call him?

"About the lying again," she said, sniffled, then added, "I can, too, do it again, when I didn't do it in the first place."

Scrambling to his feet, Ben paced the length of his room in nothing but the briefs he'd worn to bed. "Lied about what?"

Alex sniffled. "I don't know."

"Then how do you know you lied?" Ben asked, raking the hair back from his eyes while he tried to make sense of the call. The tension in the back of his neck moved down his spine. Something was very wrong.

"Pete said so," Alex said, her voice little more than a whine.

Ben rubbed his neck. "What exactly did he say?"

"That I lied."

"About what, Al?" He could hardly keep the frustration from his voice. What the hell was going on? He and Alex had never had problems communicating before.

"I don't know."

"What did he say you lied about?" Ben stared out his bedroom window to the quiet street below.

"He didn't say about anything. He just keeps saying I lied." She started to cry again. "Help me, Daddy."

He was trying, dammit. "What were you doing when he told you not to lie?" he asked.

"Hugging the wall."

"Hugging the wall?" What in hell did that mean? "Why were you doing that?"

"I was just doing like you said, Daddy. I was being brave."

"And hugging the wall is brave?"

"Uh-huh." The words turned into a tiny wail. Followed by another hiccup.

"What was Pete doing?" Ben asked. God help him, he couldn't refer to the man as Alex's father.

"Spanking me."

"*What?*" Ben's whole body went rigid, and his voice was stronger than he'd intended.

"Daaaddddyyy," Alex wailed, crying harder. "I'm s-s-sorry."

"No, Al," Ben said, forcing himself to be calm. "I'm the one who's sorry. I shouldn't have yelled."

All he could hear were sniffles and hiccups.

"Can you tell Daddy more, Al?" he asked. "Like how can you hug a wall and be spanked at the same time?"

"H-h-he spanks yucky, Daddy."

Temples throbbing, Ben took a deep breath. "How is it yucky, baby?"

And dear God, was she safe right now? What if someone walked in and found her talking to him? Would she be "spanked" again?

"H-h-he s-spanks my back, and I j-just hug the wall and be brave l-like you told me."

He was going to be sick.

"Does he spank you more than once?" Ben practically choked on the words.

"Uh-huh."

"How many times?" He was going to kill the bastard.

"I don't know, but sometimes, Daddy, I couldn't hug the wall anymore and then I cried. Are you mad at me, too, Daddy?"

"No!" Ben took another deep breath, softened his voice. "I love you, Al. Always. You know that."

"Okay." She was crying quietly.

"Where's Mommy and Pete now?"

"'Cross the street. I'm s'posed to be sleeping, only, I rolled over and my back hurts and it woke me up."

Damn them to hell. Beyond hell.

Swallowing bile, Ben tried to think, to find the most helpful thing to say. "Listen to me, Al," he began, hoping the words would come. "First, you did right by calling me, okay?"

"Okay."

"I mean that, Alex. You are always to call me when things don't seem right to you. Understand?"

"Yes, Daddy."

Okay.

"Now, I want you to climb back into bed before Mommy gets home so she's not mad that you're out of bed, okay?"

"Okay."

"And you aren't a bad girl, baby, no matter who

tells you differently. You and me, we know what a good girl you are, don't we?''

She started to cry again. ''Yeaaahh.''

Damn.

''I'm going to take care of this, Al,'' he swore to her, and to himself. He had no idea how, but he would protect Alex with his life, if it came to that.

''Can you come live in the extra room?'' she asked, her little voice weak.

''I don't think that's the answer,'' he told her, then wondered if he should've let her hold on to that particular illusion, since it seemed to give her some hope. ''It might take me a little while, but I'll fix this, Alex, I promise.''

She hiccuped.

''I've never broken a promise to you, have I, Al?''

''Uh-uh.''

''Okay, then,'' he said, rubbing the bridge of his nose. ''Just know that I'll be working to make things better, and in the meantime, you call me every chance you get.''

He had to hear from her. To know what was happening. But dear God, was he, by asking her to call, encouraging her to take a chance on getting caught? And beaten for that, as well?

''Okay.''

''And stay away from Pete as much as you can, you hear me, baby? Not if he calls you, of course— you don't want to make him mad—but otherwise, play in your room as much as you can. Will you do that for me, sweetie? Or maybe play next door?''

''Okay.''

''I love you, Al.''

''I love you, too, Daddy.'' She sounded defeated, the complete antithesis of the vivacious, precocious little girl he'd raised.

''You're being very brave, and I'm proud of you.''

''Okay.''

''You go to bed now, Al.''

''Okay.''

''Bye.'' He couldn't bear to put down the phone. To sever his only connection to her.

''Daddy?'' she said, and he wondered if she was feeling the same. His poor fragile, frightened baby girl.

''Yeah?''

''Hurry…''

She hung up before he could make the promise that was on his lips. One he wasn't sure he'd be able to keep.

BEN WAS DIFFERENT that whole first week of November. Tory couldn't put her finger on anything in particular that was wrong. He still walked with her after class. Still participated in discussions. She just didn't feel surrounded by his warmth.

Maybe she'd turned him off last Friday night, telling him about the car accident, about Christine's death. She'd introduced too much reality. The kind of bitter reality that went hand in hand with her life. She could understand his having a problem with that.

She found it overwhelming herself.

"I probably shouldn't ask, but do you think we could get a cup of coffee?" Ben met her after class the second Monday in November.

If she hadn't just been puzzling over his changed attitude, Tory would have refused immediately. "I g-guess," she said, instead. It was less than a month before term ended. A cup of coffee couldn't hurt.

"The ice-cream shop downtown has a new espresso machine. Can we meet there at, say, three o'clock?"

Her last class ended at two.

"Sure," she said tentatively.

"Thanks."

She had several hours to reconsider. Half the day, at least. But she wasn't going to. Not after that last glance Ben sent her way before striding off to his next class. He was really disturbed about something.

IF SHE'D KNOWN she was going to the ice-cream shop after school, Tory might have worn something other than the navy skirt and short matching jacket she had on. Even in Christine's low navy pumps, she felt horribly out of place.

Ben, on the other hand, fit right in, she noticed as he stood up from the red leather and Formica booth he'd chosen at the back of the shop. He wore another pair of the tight-fitting jeans he seemed to live in and a long-sleeved forest-green shirt. Even in the loose shirt, his upper body looked massive enough to shoulder whatever burdens might land there.

"What would you like?" he asked, meeting her at the counter. He already had a cup sitting in front of him at the booth.

"You go ahead," Tory said, waving toward the booth. "I'll get mine."

He seemed about to argue, but changed his mind. With a nod, he returned to the booth which was as far away from the video-game machines as possible. It might be mid-November, but the ice-cream shop was doing a steady business. Shelter Valley had been teetering around eighty-five degrees all week, and this close to the end of term, the college students seemed even more high-spirited than usual. A crowd was gathered around the video machines.

Tory ordered her coffee, said hello to one of the students in her Tuesday and Thursday afternoon American literature class, and then joined Ben at his table.

"So what's up?" she asked right away. She'd been playing guessing games since he'd walked away from her that morning. Surely he didn't have to drop out of school. Not when he was doing so well.

She'd already made up her mind that if he was having financial problems, she'd find a way to help him. One thing Tory had plenty of was money. Bruce had granted her a generous allowance, and she'd been siphoning money off to Christine for years for the times Tory escaped from him and couldn't access her own funds.

"I think Alex's new father is beating her."

Tory stared at him. "What makes you think so?"

Raucous noises at the video machines, the sounds of ice-cream scoops being dropped in cleaning bins, parents asking children what they wanted—it all faded as Tory soaked up every word Ben was telling her. Soon the ice-cream shop didn't even exist. Tory was there with little Alex, hugging that wall.

"...I called Mary the next morning, but I had to be careful," Ben was saying, running his fingers through his thick curls. "I don't want to do or say anything that might come back on Alex."

"Do you think Mary knows Pete's hitting her?"

"I didn't want to think so, but probably." He sighed, pushed his nearly full cup of coffee away. "She defends the bastard, won't hear anything negative. Says it's just sour grapes and that I'm trying to make trouble for her. That I'm jealous and bitter and don't want her to be happy."

Folding her hands in her lap to still their shaking, Tory applied herself one hundred percent to the problem. There had to be something they could do.

"Have you called the authorities?" She couldn't believe she was even asking. The authorities had become a standing joke to her and Christine. But unlike Tory, Alex had someone out there who loved her. Someone who'd back her when the adults in question used their positions, their rights as her parents, to knock holes in her story.

Ben nodded, his face ashen. "They're keeping an eye on things, but so far there's no evidence. They checked Alex at school and there's no sign of any bruises."

"They'll keep checking, I hope?"

"I don't know how involved Child Welfare's going to be, but the school nurse assured me she'd keep a close eye on Alex. She encouraged me to call her daily, which I've been doing. Apparently Al's teacher has noticed a change in her behavior. Al's not participating in class as much, doesn't seem as focused."

Tory squeezed her hands tighter together. "And Child Protective Services doesn't see that as a sign to believe her about the abuse?"

"They said it could just as easily be indicative of the change in her family structure. She needs time to adjust. They even hinted that perhaps the stories Alex is telling me are just that—stories—made up in a desperate attempt to get me back in her life."

"The bastards."

Tory could still remember the helplessness she'd felt when Massachusetts Child Welfare had found reasons to overlook her stepfather's abuse. There'd been periods when he hadn't been abusive and so there'd been no bruises, and he'd been so convincingly loving, so openly attentive at all the right times. Involved in school functions, a churchgoer, a hard worker—and Tory and Christine were just having trouble adjusting to the tragic death of their mother, they said.

Yeah. Right.

Ben looked up at her, his expression grim. "I know she's telling me the truth. Al wouldn't lie to me."

Tory nodded. "I believe you."

Tears glistened in his too-bright eyes. "She was crying like a cornered animal, dammit."

Tory felt the sensation so vividly she was sick to her stomach. "She's lucky she has you," she whispered.

The man was truly a miracle—even to a woman who didn't believe in miracles. He was the guardian angel she'd once imagined, for another child, yes, but still a guardian angel. Christine wasn't going to believe this. Tory had to tell her—

No.

She wouldn't be talking this over with Christine. Not this or anything else. When would she ever get it? When would these moments of reaching for her sister end?

Ben glanced over his shoulder at the other customers in the ice-cream shop—none of whom were paying the slightest attention to the couple sequestered in the back booth—and then at Tory. "I'm thinking about going after her," he said.

CHAPTER ELEVEN

"WHAT?" TORY SAT straight up.

"I can't just leave her there. Who knows what that bastard will do to her?"

Tory knew. But... "You can't just take her."

"Like hell I can't." His eyes were hard as flint, his hands in tight fists on the table.

"And then what?" she asked quietly. "What kind of life would you be able to give her?"

"A loving one."

"Yes, but it'll be a life on the run, which is no life at all." Tory could vouch for that. "She'd be living a lie, never able to make friends...or to love anyone but you."

Ben didn't budge, his chin jutting, his jaw tense. "I'm not saying it would be perfect, but it's got to be better than what she has now."

"For a time, maybe," Tory said. She'd sure done her share of dreaming as a kid, before she'd given up on dreams. Her favorite had been the one where her real father came back, full of love and explanations and apologies, and stole her and Christine away from the bastard who was raising them.

"But chances are good you'd be caught eventually," she said, knowing that firsthand, too. "And you'll be an outlaw, tried, and probably sent to jail. Alex will then be returned to her parents, who'll most likely blame her for the entire debacle and punish her accordingly. And this time you won't be around to help her."

"It's been almost two weeks since she called," he said, his shoulders slumped. His hands were still clenched, as though ready to hit someone. "And what help have I been to her so far?"

"The right kind," Tory said, desperate to assure him. The fact that he loved Alex, that he was pulling for her, that he cared so deeply, was the best gift he could give the little girl. It was a gift Tory had prayed for all her life.

"I promised her."

"And you're keeping that promise," she said strongly, almost tempted to reach out and cover one of those clenched fists with her hand. "You're in constant contact with people who see her five days a week, who're watching out for her. Those are the people who'll know exactly what to do if anything happens again." She crossed her fingers under the table.

Please, Chrissie, if you're up there, protect little Alex. Please don't let her end up like us.

Ben wrapped his hands around his cold cup of coffee and studied Tory for a long moment.

"You sound like an authority on this stuff," he said assessingly.

Face hot, Tory made herself breathe. And think.

"I, uh, I'm a teacher." She found the answer from somewhere. "We're trained to know these things."

He frowned. "But you teach college. Child abuse is hardly a problem in your classroom."

"True." She licked her lips. "But my undergraduate degree was in education." The truth saved her. Sort of. It was Christine's truth, not hers, but then, it was Christine sitting there with Ben.

However, it was Tory who was starting to care about him.

OVER THE NEXT WEEK and a half, Christine became a lifeline for Ben. She kept him sane. If not for her, he'd for sure have gone off half-cocked to California, kidnapped his daughter and run.

To what, he didn't know. A lifetime of dead-end jobs, of no relationships other than with Alex. Still, it might've been worth it to get the constant worm of worry out of his gut. To know that his precious child was safe.

But Christine was right. If they ever got caught, Al's life would be over. She'd be given back to Mary and the bastard, and there'd be no way he could save her a second time. Not from prison. As much as he hated it, he had to bide his time, play by the rules and pray that right would win.

So he lived for the moments each day when he could call the nurse at Alex's school, lived for the report that Al was in class and wasn't bruised. And the rest of the time, he studied. Final exams were coming up in a couple of weeks, and he had a perfect grade point going. He was hoping to get some scholarship money to offset the loans he'd arranged for the remainder of his education.

And he lived for the hour or so each Monday, Wednesday and Friday morning when he was with Christine. Her eyes always asked about Alex the moment she saw him in class. And then filled with obvious relief when he nodded that everything was okay.

On their walks back to her office after class, she continued to buoy up his strength, his decision to stay where he was. He knew almost nothing about the woman, and yet she was becoming his mainstay.

He knew almost nothing, yet he sensed a great deal. Although she was more relaxed around him since that day at the ice-cream shop, she was frequently still uncomfortable—especially that time he'd accidentally bumped into her while they were walking after class. She'd jumped as though she'd been shot.

He vowed to himself that someday, when he was no longer her student and she was no longer his teacher, when things with Alex were as they should be, he was going to find out why Christine Evans was so frightened of him.

Someday. When he could attend to the answer.

"Are you doing anything special for Thanksgiving tomorrow?" Christine asked hesitantly as Ben walked with her across the campus after class.

Actually Zack had invited him over for dinner with his partner, Cassie, and her parents, but he'd declined. He hadn't felt up to a family gathering. Not without Alex.

"Buddy and I are planning to lie around and get fat," he told her. In reality, he planned to study. Exercise. Take the dog for a long walk. Watch some football. Anything to keep his mind off Alex and what kind of holiday she might be having. He was afraid it meant the bastard would be home all day— and that Alex would be in more danger because of that.

He prayed his little girl would remember to stay in her room as much as she could.

And hated to think of her alone in there, playing all by herself.

"Buddy?" Christine asked, frowning. And then, "Oh, yeah, you mentioned him once before. He's your dog, right?"

"If you can call him that. He's not convinced of it yet."

She smiled one of her rare, unfettered smiles. She looked breathtakingly beautiful. "What does he think he is?"

"My boss."

"Oh." Her smile faded. "Well, Phyllis, um, suggested that if you aren't doing anything, you might want to come by for Thanksgiving dinner with us."

She moved a little farther away from him on the wide sidewalk that cut across the middle of campus.

"I guess it's kind of a common practice at Montford," she added, "for teachers with families to invite students who aren't going home. The administration doesn't want any students to spend the holiday alone, unless they choose to. Will and Becca usually have a houseful themselves, except I'm not sure they are this year, with Bethany and all...." Her voice trailed off.

Ben wasn't hot about the idea of being a needy student for the holiday.

But dinner with Christine was more of a temptation than he could currently withstand. Just being with her would help him fight off the demons that would prey on his mind this first Thanksgiving without his daughter.

"What time should I be there?"

ARMED WITH A TUB of port-wine cheese and a bottle of white zinfandel, Ben showed up promptly at two the next afternoon at the address Christine had given him. He wasn't sure how formal the occasion was supposed to be, so he'd worn a pair of black pants and a white button-down oxford shirt, figuring the clothes would cover any eventuality.

He was glad he'd made the effort when Christine opened the door wearing a simple but casually elegant navy-and-white silk jumpsuit. Her hair was stylishly windblown about her shoulders, allowing, as she moved, brief glimpses of the double gold hoops in her ears.

"You look beautiful," he said before he remembered she was his teacher and he wasn't supposed to say things like that.

"Thank you."

She wouldn't meet his eyes.

"Ben, hi!" Phyllis came up behind Christine. "We're glad you could make it."

Ben smiled at the other woman, handing over his gifts. "I'm glad you asked me," he told her.

And he was. Other than with Alex, he couldn't think of anyplace he'd rather be. Certainly not home alone with only a dog to share his meal, as he'd been planning.

Phyllis Langford was a born nurturer. Within five minutes of his arrival, Ben was feeling completely at home, in the kitchen carving the turkey while Phyllis mashed potatoes and Christine stood at the stove making gravy.

"Becca told me something interesting last night when I was over there for dinner," Phyllis said, pouring milk into the big stainless pot she'd used to cook the potatoes.

Ben glanced up from the bird he was carving, the electric knife suspended.

"She thinks you're entitled to half of Montford Mansion," she said.

"Your kidding!" Christine stopped stirring and stared at Phyllis.

"What makes her think that?" Ben asked, back at his carving.

"Apparently your great-grandfather's will—and all subsequent ones—stipulate that the estate is to remain in the possession of any living Montford heirs. It doesn't name names, just says the heirs. That's you."

"And Sam," Christine added.

Turning on the portable mixer, Phyllis nodded. "Sam Montford IV," she said. "Did Becca tell you how he left town about ten years ago and nobody's heard from him since? Not even his parents."

"His parents own Montford Mansion now, right?" Christine asked.

"They're the ones in possession of it," Phyllis said, her voice raised over the mixer. "But from what I understand, no one's lived there for almost two years. No one knows for sure why they left, but Becca said the speculation is that it's because of Sam. His continued absence was breaking their hearts." She turned off the mixer. "Sam's ex-wife, Cassie, came back to town shortly after they left."

"Is she Zack's partner?" Ben asked. He thought so, but no one had ever said, and he hadn't asked. Becca hadn't gotten that far the night he'd been over there for dinner. Little Bethany had cut the evening short.

Phyllis nodded, detached the beaters and put them in the sink. "She's a veterinarian, too, a nice girl, pretty, super smart, but I guess she keeps to herself a lot. When Becca was trying to find Sam for her Fourth of July celebration, Cassie told her she hadn't heard from him in years."

"I know Zack," Ben said, his knife whirring on and off as he carved. "But I've never met Cassie. She seems to travel a lot."

"She's a genius with pet therapy," Phyllis told them. "She's known all over the country, has had amazing results. She gets calls all the time from desperate people who are sure she can help them.''

Sounded to Ben like his cousin was a total loser, leaving a woman like that. "Does she? Help them, I mean?" he asked.

"Yeah," Phyllis said, wrapping the cord back around the mixer. "What I hear from Will and Becca is that more often than not, she does help, often with the mentally ill, sick kids and so on. I'm hoping to spend some time with her myself later on. I'm really fascinated by what she's been able to accomplish."

"So does anyone know where the Montfords are?" Christine asked, stirring a little more flour into the gravy.

Putting the mixer under the cupboard, Phyllis stood. "They're in Europe someplace."

"So that house just sits there empty?" Christine stopped stirring again to look at Phyllis.

"They have someone come in to clean once a month. Becca thinks they might be coming home for the holidays, though. Apparently the woman who cleans the place heard from them recently. They want her to have food in the refrigerator the third week in December."

Ben's heart quickened while he listened silently. Becca had told him about his aunt and uncle when he'd gone to dinner that night. He'd been thinking about them, envisioning himself telling them that he existed—and was in town. He just wasn't ready to do it yet.

He wasn't sure he had what it took to be a Montford in Shelter Valley. He was no wealthy patriarch. He was a manual laborer who wanted nothing more than to get an education—and to gain custody of the daughter who wasn't even his.

"I think you should meet them," Christine said, looking briefly in his direction, smiling ever so slightly.

The electric knife slid off the turkey's breast, leaving him with a few shavings, rather than a decent slice of meat.

He amended his previous thought. He did want something more. He wanted to get to know his teacher in a way that students didn't normally get to do.

All it took was one smile from her to give him a jolt.

"Maybe someday," he answered her. When he had a college degree under his belt. When Alex's life was settled in a manner that satisfied him.

"You deserve your share of the inheritance," Phyllis offered, dipping her finger into the potatoes for a taste.

He sliced a leg off the turkey, putting it on the platter whole. "I'm doing all right without it," he said. "I have more of an interest in getting to know my family—in *having* family—than I am in collecting a share of something that was never mine to begin with."

Christine sent him a sideways glance, one he

would have missed completely if he wasn't so damned aware of every move she made.

"Just because you didn't know about it doesn't mean it wasn't yours," Phyllis reasoned.

"You'd really give up a chance to live on the hill?" Christine asked, referring to the mountain where Becca and Will Parsons lived.

"In a second."

Whether that raised him or lowered him in her eyes didn't change his answer. "I want nice things in life as much as the next guy," he explained, "but I have no problem working for them. I'd actually prefer to gain them that way." It was part of his Indian heritage, he guessed, but Ben didn't want handouts.

Even ancestral ones.

"You wouldn't have to worry about school loans," Christine said, watching him now.

He grinned at her. "You've got a point. But I'll manage. I'm hoping my grades will earn me some scholarship money."

Her gaze continued to hold his for another couple of seconds, long enough to be obvious, and Ben was pleasantly surprised to read admiration there.

"You two going to finish fixing dinner or am I eating potatoes and salad all by myself?" Phyllis finally asked.

"There's enough turkey here for dinner," Ben said as Christine turned away. "I can finish carving the leftovers after we eat."

"The gravy's done," Christine poured it into a

gravy boat, then took the long way around to the table, to avoid getting too close to him. He might have been put off if that smile, that look he'd seen in her eyes, wasn't still warming his insides.

The woman was a mystery that continued to draw him in. In spite of the fact that her hands-off sign was bigger than she was.

The sign didn't bother him much. He had no intention of getting seriously involved again until he had Alex settled. And until he had an education and a job he enjoyed, a job that would support whatever responsibilities he might create. Right now, he just wanted to get to know Christine. To find the source of her shadows. To understand why he frightened her sometimes. To be her friend.

Not to get involved.

LATER THAT NIGHT, Tory and Phyllis were in the kitchen, emptying the dishwasher. Ben had left a short while before, having stayed to watch *Miracle on Thirty-Fourth Street* with them—Phyllis's choice, a family tradition of hers—and then they'd all enjoyed slices of pumpkin pie Phyllis had made.

"If you live to be a hundred, you're never going to meet a guy as great as Ben Sanders," Phyllis said when she was standing at the silverware drawer—a safe distance from Tory—with a full bin of silverware to sort through and put away. She didn't need to spend a lot of time with the younger man to recognize his worth, his fundamental decency. The way he talked about his daughter. His lack of avarice toward the Montford fortune. Most of all, what he brought out in Tory.

"If I live to be a hundred, I'm more cursed than I thought," Tory said. She was tending to the pans.

Tory had changed out of her jumpsuit as soon as Ben went home, putting on a pair of dark sweats and an old T-shirt, her usual around-the-house outfit. No woman should be able to wear such shapeless clothes and still look so good, Phyllis thought. If she didn't care for Tory so darn much, she'd hate her.

Phyllis was still wearing the pantsuit she'd had on all day. Mostly because she actually felt good in it. It was new, and complimented her slimmer body— slimmer by twelve pounds.

"You're attracted to him," she said, her instincts telling her that if she didn't push, Tory might lose this chance she'd been waiting a lifetime to find. The chance to be part of a healthy, loving, maybe even exciting relationship.

"I am not."

"Then why did you doll yourself up for him?"

"I was married to Bruce for a lot of years. Etiquette for entertaining is ingrained." Tory moved to the glasses, setting them on the shelf above the dishwasher.

"And that's why you got jittery anytime he came too close?"

"You know why I'm not comfortable around men." Her voice was muffled by the cupboard door as she returned a stack of plates.

"But you aren't afraid of Ben, are you?" Phyllis

asked. Even if Tory never went on a date with Ben, never gave him a chance, she at least had to see that she could be around a man and not feel instant fear.

Finishing with the plates, Tory left the question unanswered.

"I saw the way you looked at him, honey," Phyllis said softly, meeting Tory at the dishwasher with the empty silverware bin.

"Stop it!" Tory said, her voice stronger than Phyllis had ever heard it. "What's the point?"

"The point is for you to see that there's hope, Tory. Maybe you can even begin to believe in some kind of future."

"Ben's just a student." Tory pushed the door of dishwasher shut with a little more force than necessary.

"So you keep telling yourself. But that excuse is only going to last another few weeks, until he's no longer your student. Then what?"

Tory leaned back against the counter, her arms folded in front of her. "Then I don't expect I'll be seeing him again."

"Shelter Valley isn't Boston, Tory. You can't get lost in the crowd here."

"That doesn't mean I have to *date* the crowd."

Phyllis's heart tore wide open when she heard the little-girl longing hidden behind the bitterness in Tory's voice. "We're only talking about one man, not a crowd."

"And again, what's the point?" Tory asked, her

gaze meeting Phyllis's, her expression one of weary resignation. "I'm dead, remember?"

Phyllis was overwhelmed with frustration at the cruel irony that now determined Tory's life. Tory had to be Christine to stay alive, but as long as she was Christine, she couldn't live.

"Someone's standing in this room with me, Tory," she finally said. "We just have to figure out who that someone is. And when we do, she'll be free to live—and even love, if she wants to."

Tory watched her for a couple of minutes and Phyllis could almost see the thoughts forming in her mind.

"No matter what the externals of the life I'm living, whether I answer to Christine or Tory, whether I'm a teacher or an ex-wife on the run, what's on the inside doesn't change," she said quietly. "And all other problems aside, I don't think the person in here—" she pounded her fist lightly against her chest "—can ever let go and live as you want her to."

Phyllis's heart sank. Tory sounded so sure. And so rational. "Why not?"

"I killed my sister. I don't deserve to live."

Oh—so it was the *guilt* they were dealing with. As long as it had a name, Phyllis could attack it.

"You didn't kill her, Tory, but I can understand why you feel as though you did, since you're the one Bruce was after when Christine died."

Tory stared at Phyllis, her gaze unflinching.

But Phyllis didn't drop her eyes, didn't look away.

"The point is, you would gladly have died in her stead if you'd had any say in the matter," she went on. "The choice wasn't yours. It was out of your hands. A stronger will—or power—than your own made that decision. You had nothing to do with Christine's death."

Tory's gaze fell, but not before Phyllis had seen the tears shining in her eyes. "I wish I could believe that."

"Believe it, Tory. It's the truth."

Tory shook her head. "It doesn't make sense."

"Would it make more sense if you'd lost your life?"

"Of course it would." Tory looked up again, her voice certain.

"And why is that?"

"Look at me," Tory said, gesturing at her body with both hands. "Not only did my stepfather mess me up, but Bruce did, too. You said it yourself. I can't even be around a man as nice as Ben Sanders and not get all jittery." The words flowed briskly now that they'd been released. "Hell, I can't even walk beside him on the sidewalk unless there's at least a foot between us. How can you think someone like that could ever live a normal life?"

"You work through the shit and get beyond it," Phyllis said.

Tory's lips twisted into a half grin. "Spoken like a true psychotherapist."

Phyllis shrugged, returning the grin. Her answer might have been coarse, but it was also true.

"I have no education, no real experience at anything worthwhile. Nothing to contribute," Tory said, her tone not self-pitying or even self-denigrating, but plainly matter-of-fact.

It brought a rush of tears to Phyllis's eyes, but she quickly blinked them away. Tory needed her to be completely focused.

"I know how to entertain, how to dress, how to do my hair and makeup, and how to run," Tory continued, ticking each item off on her fingers.

"You know how to be kind and thoughtful," Phyllis rebutted immediately. "You help me around here in a million little ways, simply because you notice that things need to be done, not because I ask you to do them. You even do my laundry."

"I have my own to do, anyway."

"You listen to people, you have an understanding of human suffering far beyond your years and the compassion to go with it. You're highly intelligent, loyal, dependable—"

"Until Bruce catches up with me again, and then I'll be gone without so much as a goodbye, leaving everything undone."

Tory wasn't ready to believe in herself yet, to separate what life had forced her to be from who she was inside. But Phyllis wasn't giving up. Not if it took them both until they were a hundred.

"Besides, Christine was all those good things, and more," Tory said. "While I ran away from home, straight into the arms of my sister's murderer, she actually made something of herself. She got a very impressive education, a worthwhile job. She was beautiful, generous, giving. She could've had any man she wanted, and he would've been the luckiest guy on earth..."

Tory's voice trailed off, and Phyllis could hear a hint of the tears she was obviously fighting.

"She had her whole life ahead of her," Tory finished in a whisper, losing her battle with tears.

And Phyllis made a decision. One she wasn't happy about. One she wasn't even sure about. But one that wasn't going to change. Christine's life was over. There was nothing more Phyllis could do for her. Tory's life was still ahead of her, whether she wanted to believe that or not. And Phyllis's training told her that sharing Christine's secret could very well be the catalyst that might help Tory find at least a modicum of peace. It might help relieve her of the heavy burden of guilt she was carrying over Christine's death. Phyllis knew, deeply and intuitively, that Christine would want her to share this hideous secret.

While Phyllis missed Christine every day, she was at peace for her friend, at peace knowing that Christine was finally free from her burdens.

But Tory didn't know about those burdens, so couldn't find that peace. She didn't know about the emptiness Christine's life would've always had. And while Phyllis wasn't Tory's therapist, she was certainly qualified to be. Without a doubt, she was as close as Tory was ever going to get to the professional counseling that would help her.

They'd been breaking the rules since this entire nightmare began. Breaking them for the right reasons. Breaking them because there was no other choice. It was time to break another one.

"Come with me. There's something I have to tell you."

CHAPTER TWELVE

TORY FOLLOWED PHYLLIS into the living room, where she sat on the floor and leaned against the sofa as Phyllis also sat on the floor, her back against the matching chair. Her friend was really looking great, even after a long day of cooking and entertaining. She had a waist now, one that was shown off quite nicely in the new pantsuit—and the royal blue was the perfect complement to Phyllis's pretty red hair. But it was the life in Phyllis's face that captivated Tory. And occasionally frightened her.

"What's up?" she asked, somewhat frightened now. Phyllis's usually smiling face was serious.

Tory's fear grew when Phyllis opened her mouth and then closed it again without speaking. She'd never seen her friend at a loss for words.

Phyllis smiled, though her smile was more nervous than comforting, and tried again. "I don't quite know how to do this."

Sitting stiffly against the couch, her back ramrod straight, her legs out in front of her, Tory waited.

"I don't know how much Christine told you about me, about our relationship..."

"She said you were the best friend she'd ever had."

Phyllis's face broke slowly into a real smile then. A smile that revealed more than a hint of tears.

"She was the best friend I'd ever had, too," she admitted, looking down at her hands. "The sister I always wanted. She talked to me, Tory, about certain things she'd never told anyone before." Phyllis looked back up at her. "Not even you."

Tory doubted there was anything about Christine she didn't know. Abuse did that to a family. Made them closer than close, made them feel each other's pain. She and Christine had always been aware of each other, known where the other one was at all times—except when Tory had started running. They'd shared everything.

But that wasn't something she'd expect Phyllis to know. It wasn't something the victims of abuse ever spoke about.

Phyllis's chin was almost on her chest as she sat propped against the chair, smoothing patterns in the carpet. "Tell me about your stepfather."

"Why?" Phyllis was supposed to be telling *her* something.

Was this some kind of psychiatrist trick to get her to talk? Was Phyllis just trying to get her to go out with Ben Sanders, who, by the way, hadn't even *asked* her out or expressed any intention of doing so in the future?

"Christine told me a lot about those years," Phyllis said. "I'd like to hear about them from you, too."

"Why?"

Tory didn't talk about her stepfather. Not ever.

That was the beauty of living with Phyllis, or part of it, anyway. This was the first time in her life that she'd been with someone other than Christine who knew what they'd been through—yet she didn't have to talk about it. She'd been shocked at first when Christine had told her that she'd confided in Phyllis about their teenage years.

Later, she'd been grateful.

"I have a reason, Tory, I promise. And I'll tell you soon, but just trust me here, okay?"

Trust. That five-letter word that was worse than any four-letter word Tory had ever heard. Because when it was broken—as Tory's had so cruelly been—it destroyed you inside.

"He drank."

"All the time?"

Tory's legs were so stiff they were cramping. "No."

"When did he drink?"

"Sometimes at night, when he got home from work. As we got older, practically all the time on weekends."

"And?" Phyllis sat up, too, her ankles crossed in front of her. Her eyes, when Tory dared to look at them, were burning with compassion.

Tory gazed down at her lap. "You already know," she said. "Christine already told you."

Phyllis nodded. "And now I'm asking *you* to tell me."

"Why?" Tory demanded again. Phyllis had never been cruel before.

Waiting until Tory glanced up, Phyllis said, "Please?"

"When he drank, he got mean." Tory delivered the words with as little thought as possible.

Survival, strength, meant staying away from those memories.

"How mean?"

Head shooting up, she glared at Phyllis. "What's with you?" she asked. "You get some kind of weird pleasure from hearing about other people's misery?"

"No," Phyllis answered calmly, but Tory glimpsed the instant of pain in her friend's eyes.

That glimpse kept Tory in the room.

"He hit us, okay?" she spit out, staring at the empty chair just over Phyllis's shoulder. "Is that what you wanted to hear?"

"It's what I expected to hear."

"So what were you going to tell me?" Tory needed a drink. Her throat was so dry it hurt.

"Is that all he did—hit you?"

"I told you our stepfather beat us. What more do you want?" Tory cried. "The details? Sometimes he used his bare hands. He'd backhand whichever one of us happened to be closest, knocking our heads against the wall until we saw stars. Sometimes he'd punch us. If we were lucky enough to have time to turn around, he'd pull off his belt and leave welts on our backs that sometimes got infected."

She stopped, tried to swallow. "Is that enough, or do you want more?"

"Is there more?"

"Of course there's more!" Tory was barely able to make the words coherent, she was shaking so badly. "There were stitches, a broken wrist, probably a couple of concussions, not that we went to the hospital to find out..."

Phyllis didn't move, didn't cringe, didn't attempt to take Tory in her arms like the counselor at school had the one time Tory had gone to her, daring to believe that help could be found there. Ashamed as she'd been, she'd waited until the bruises had healed. And with no evidence and a stepfather who was active in the local parent-teacher organization, who volunteered his services for homecoming festivities, who served on church committees and who testified that both Christine and Tory were having a difficult time adjusting to their mother's death—there'd been no help. The most Tory had received from the ordeal was a hug that had almost sent her out of her skin.

"Other than the beatings, did he ever do anything else?"

It wasn't a question Tory had been expecting. "Sure, he supported us financially, cooked dinner when he was sober, carpooled once in a while." Unless you'd lived with her stepfather, seen the change from kind to cruel when he was slapping you silly, you'd never understand why all the nice things he'd done had only made the situation worse.

Phyllis continued to prod Tory until she'd listed every good deed she could think of—and every bad one. By the time she was done, she'd never felt so drained in her life. Not even after the days of endless driving and crying for her dead sister.

"And that's all," Phyllis finally said, pulling herself into a fully sitting position.

"Probably not, but it's all I can remember." Dry-eyed, Tory felt as if she was going to throw up.

Phyllis ran both hands through her hair, then rubbed them along her legs.

"Christine remembered more."

Confused, exhausted, Tory threw up her hand and let it drop. "Of course she would. She's older than me." She stopped, bit her lip. "She *was* older than me."

It had been months, and she still couldn't think of Christine in the past tense. Maybe that was partly because every day when she went to work, Christine still lived.

"Tory, your stepfather raped Christine."

Tory's heart froze. "He did not." How could Phyllis even say something so horrible? Wasn't what she and Christine had been through enough? God, she felt sick.

And sicker as she noticed the tears filling Phyllis's eyes. "Yes, honey, he did. Many times."

"No!" Violently pushing herself off the floor, Tory stood up. "You take that back! You know it's not true," she said, turning blindly toward the archway that led into the hall. Then she turned around. "Take that back."

Phyllis was still on the floor where Tory had left her, but sitting as though she was in a strait-jacket. Part of Tory wondered how hard it was for Phyllis to make herself sit there. She suspected it was really hard.

"I can't, honey," Phyllis whispered, her eyes filled with anguish.

"It's not true," Tory told her, certain of that. She had to be certain. She couldn't even consider the alternative.

But she didn't leave. She couldn't let Phyllis just stay there, sitting like that. "Why don't you get up and sit on the couch," she asked, coming a couple of steps back into the room. "You'll be more comfortable."

"I'm fine here," Phyllis said, tears dripping slowly down her face.

"No, I'm sure the couch would be more comfortable." Tory reached for a tissue, and leaned close enough to Phyllis to hand it to her, careful that their fingers didn't touch.

She couldn't get that close. Those vile words had come from Phyllis.

"Thank you," Phyllis said softly, wiping her face.

"Please get up on the couch," Tory tried again. If she could just get Phyllis comfortable, she could leave.

The Mustang needed gas. Or if it didn't, it should.

There wouldn't be a station open in Shelter Valley, not this late and not on Thanksgiving, but if she drove into Phoenix she'd be able to find an all-night convenience store with gas pumps.

"She was thirteen the first time it happened."

Tory was shaking so hard she couldn't stand any longer. Sinking to the floor, she slipped deep inside herself, not sure she was strong enough to listen. Not sure she was strong enough to know.

She was going to sit there for a few minutes, just until her legs quit shaking so much. And then she'd stand up and walk right out of this room. Out of this house.

"I think he killed something inside Christine that day, something that had managed to survive all the beatings. But it couldn't survive that kind of violence."

"No!" Tory said, her hands over her ears as, face lowered, she shook her head back and forth. "No, no, no."

"She couldn't bear to have you find out. And more, couldn't bear to let him kill the little bit of innocence, the soul, that was left intact inside you…"

Christine thought she had soul left?

"She tried at first to report him, but you two had already been so humiliated when they hadn't believed you about the beatings and…and he swore he'd say Christine had seduced him. She was afraid they'd send her away and leave you alone with him. The damage had already been done to her, and at that point, her only goal was to protect you from the same fate. She made sure she kept him…satisfied so he wouldn't turn to you. She never left you alone in the house with him after that."

Christine *had* always been home, but that was because when she went to the university, her classes happened to get out earlier than Tory's high-school classes did. And she didn't date because she was studying. How else could she have received her doctorate at such a young age?

How else could she have earned her freedom?

"She told me that her only reason for staying alive was to protect you, to see that you had a decent life, to see you happy."

"She had lots of things to live for," Tory said, her hands still over her ears, eyes closed, her head almost in her lap. "She loved her job."

"She loved you," Phyllis told her. "And maybe, there at the end, she learned to trust and care about me some, too. Everything else was just a means to an end."

"No, it wasn't," Tory insisted. "She just hadn't met the right man, one she could trust." She looked up at Phyllis. "It's hard to trust a man after you've been beaten by the one you lived with as a kid," she informed her.

Phyllis might have read enough books, worked on enough studies, had enough clinical experience, to be considered an expert, but there were some things nothing could prepare you for.

She held Tory's gaze steadily.

"Once Chrissie met the right man, she would've settled down with him, had a family, been happy," Tory went on. "Christine was born to be a mother. Look how well she looked after me."

Phyllis shook her head. "She couldn't have children."

Tory didn't say a word. She felt the blood drain away from her face, from her hands, but she couldn't move. She was immobile, a deer in front of headlights, waiting to be hit again. She'd been there before. Many times.

"She got pregnant and was terrified what your stepfather would do if he found out," Phyllis continued, but the words were obviously costing her. Each one came out sounding tearful, choked.

"She went to a clinic where they didn't require any signatures."

"Ohhh…" Tory moaned, rocking herself. For someone who was no stranger to pain, she'd never known she could hurt so badly.

"She said the doctor was nice to her, but after several days of bleeding, she knew something was wrong. By the time she went for help, it was too late. They had to do a hysterectomy."

"Where was I?" Tory asked, looking up, her head feeling as though it was stuffed with cotton. "If she'd had surgery I would have known about it." This whole terrible thing was a mistake. They weren't talking about *her* Christine. Phyllis had her confused with someone else.

"You remember when she had her appendix out?" Phyllis asked quietly.

Tory closed her eyes again. *Oh, God.* She opened them. Looked at Phyllis and crumpled. Her shoulders, her ribs, her spine, everything just gave out on her.

It was true. The entire vile story was true.

With superhuman strength, Tory made it to her feet, managed to stumble out the door and to the bathroom in time to lose every bit of her Thanksgiving dinner.

Her poor, beloved, tortured sister.

THE TIMING of Phyllis's revelation about Christine turned out to be a blessing in that the holiday gave Tory three full days to pull herself together before she had to resume teaching. Before she had to pretend that everything was still the same, that nothing had changed.

"Some people would be able to survive what Christine went through and find some measure of happiness here on earth," Phyllis had told her over the weekend. "Christine's spirit was too tender...."

And another time, she'd said, "Christine's only goal was to find a way for you to be happy. Perhaps she's done that now...."

Tory wasn't so sure, but as she prepared for class on Monday morning, Phyllis's words continued to replay themselves in her mind. And somehow, over the next week, as she adjusted to the horror of Christine's rape, she also found a slight respite from the horrible guilt that had been crippling her with every breath she took and Christine didn't.

Are you happier now, Chrissie?

Phyllis thought she was.

Tory didn't have an answer.

CHAPTER THIRTEEN

THE THURSDAY AFTER Thanksgiving, Ben was enjoying the balmy seventy-degree weather as he walked across Montford's still-green campus. The combination of grass and cactus was unnatural, in his opinion, and he found the lack of fall trees, plus the abundance of palm trees, saguaro cactus and golf-course-green grass a bit odd so close to Christmas. In Flagstaff and northern California, where he'd spent most of his life, there were four seasons and the usual foliage or lack thereof that accompanied them.

With a manila envelope under his arm, both hands in the pockets of his jeans, he turned toward Christine's office building with more lift in his step than he'd had in a while.

He wasn't sure she'd be there, though this was part of her scheduled office hours. She'd seemed a bit more distracted than usual this past week; he wondered if maybe she was busy with end-of-term meetings and other administrative stuff.

The thought that she might be rebuilding emotional walls they'd managed to break down on Thanksgiving had crossed his mind. But it didn't deter him. He couldn't shake the feeling that Christine desperately needed a friend. And that, for some reason he didn't understand, he'd been chosen.

He also couldn't deny that being with her made his burdens a little easier to bear.

If she needed space now and then, that was fine with him. He needed space, too—had goals to meet before he intended to even think about making another emotional investment. Before he even considered the possibility of remarriage.

Ben was a patient man. After years of living with Mary, he knew what mattered in a relationship—friendship—and recognized some of that genuine, honest awareness between him and Christine. Recognized it because he'd lived without it for so long.

And because neither of them particularly wanted it.

Light was shining under her door. Good. She was there.

"Come in," she called in answer to his knock.

He did, swinging her door almost shut behind him. "You busy?" he asked.

She pushed away a pile of papers and looked up at him, her eyes tired. "Not really." The smile she gave him wasn't quite relaxed, but not as nervous as it had been several weeks ago. "Just getting a head start on the weekend—grading essays."

"You really bleed over them, don't you," he said. He'd seen the number of comments—complimentary and constructive—she'd made, not only on his essays but on those of his classmates.

"I guess I do." She shrugged. "If you guys are going to put in the time and thought and effort to write these papers, you deserve to have time spent on my end, too, don't you think?"

Ben nodded. Then he slid the envelope he'd been carrying in front of her. "This came yesterday. Open it," he said, standing back, hands in his pockets once again.

With a curious glance at him, she turned her attention to the envelope, pulled out the single sheet, read it—and grinned up at him. The first honest-to-goodness, genuine, completely unforced expression he'd ever seen on her face.

In that moment, she seemed about twenty, not the thirty he knew her to be.

"Congratulations!" she said, looking at the paper again.

Ben rocked back on his heels. "I came to thank you," he told her. "If you hadn't encouraged me to submit the paper to begin with, I'd never have thought of it."

"And now you're going to be published!"

"In the December issue."

"It says here you have to sign a release form."

"Already done. Mailed it this morning."

"And you get ten free copies of the publication. I hope you'll autograph one for me."

"Sure." Still too pleased with himself to feel embarrassed, Ben smiled. "You're a great teacher, Christine." He wasn't sure where that had come from, hadn't planned to sound as though he was buttering up his teacher. But the words were true, and she seemed so hesitant at times. Like just now, when he'd thanked her.

Christine slid the paper back into the envelope, then refastened the clasp and handed it to him. "You've already got an A, Sanders. The flattery's not necessary," she said.

"Hey!" He grabbed her hand as he took the envelope and waited for her to look at him.

When she did, her eyes were wary. He was also surprised to notice that her hand was shaking.

"You know me better than that," he said, trying to find the connection they'd shared the week before.

She jerked her hand and he let go. She was, after all, his teacher. And they were in her office.

But it wasn't always going to be that way.

THE LAST TWO WEEKS of classes were busy ones for Tory as she crammed every moment with preparing for her daily lessons and grading several hundred end-of-term papers, as well as quietly researching previous exams in American Literature 101. And then preparing her own exam. For once, something worked to her advantage, as her eighteen-hour days left little time for introspection. And made her too tired to lie awake at night.

She had no opportunity to fret over her reaction to Ben Sanders those weeks, although he was always there, a constant reminder of a life she could never live. He still walked her to her office after class, and many times those few minutes of conversation were the highlight of her day. Not that she'd admit it to anyone. She even tried to keep that acknowledgment from herself.

Any closeness between them was a mistake. Got them nowhere.

Ben continued to be in contact with Alex's school, but there was nothing to report. No change in Alex's withdrawn behavior. But no bruises, either. Tory waited for those reports. And listened to them with a mixture of relief and dread.

She was always shaking when Ben left her after those conversations.

He hadn't heard from Alex himself since that last terrible conversation almost six weeks before.

Tory wasn't sure that was good news, although she didn't mention her suspicions to Ben. She had a feeling he figured the same thing, but he didn't voice it, either.

Then, suddenly, classes were over. Exams were held and graded, and her first semester as a college professor was successfully completed. She turned in her grades, locked Christine's office door and left Montford University for the month-long Christmas break.

And everything that had been pushed away for the end-of-school rush came flooding back. It hadn't disappeared as she'd tried to pretend, but had been right there waiting all along.

Could she do it again? Head into another semester living a lie? Did she have any other choice?

Would she ever get the obscene vision of her step-father and Christine out of her mind? Or her heart?

How was she going to make it through Christmas without Christine? Or the rest of her life, for that matter.

Were the holidays going to bring more trouble for little Alex? Tory had never understood it, but abuse always seemed to get worse around the jolliest time of the year. She lay awake in bed more than one night thinking of Ben's little girl, sending silent prayers to a God she no longer believed in. She hoped with everything in her that the child would be all right.

And she tried desperately not to relive her own hellish holidays of the past. Not to see those years with a new vile slant. Not to know that Christine had suffered even more than *she* had.

During the days, Tory kept busy. She helped Phyllis decorate for Christmas, ran errands for her friend, washed all the curtains and bedspreads and offered to wrap gifts for the needy-family Christmas drive Becca Parsons had organized.

Phyllis had told her that Becca was on the Shelter Valley Town Council but that she wasn't returning to work until January because she wanted to be home with her baby. That didn't mean Becca wasn't working, though. She still worked with Save the Youth and with a number of committees, and she ran the Christmas-gift campaign, which was partic-ularly close to her heart. If the number of presents Tory had to wrap were any indication, Becca's fund-

raising was as skillful as Phyllis had said. And her
generosity as limitless.

Despite her full schedule, Tory often thought
about her visits with Ben. She tried not to, but she
did. Class was over. She'd known she wouldn't be
seeing him again after finals week. Was actually
glad of that.

And yet, dammit, she missed him. Missed their
conversations. Missed being close to him even if she
had had to keep the entire sidewalk between them.
He made her nervous as hell—and she missed him.

On Friday morning, the second week in December, Tory stacked the wrapped toys and clothes in
the trunk of her Mustang, on the backseat and on
the passenger seat. They'd taken up less room when
she'd brought them all home in bags.

She wrote a note for Phyllis, who was over at
Martha Moore's house helping Martha put up a
Christmas tree—and probably bolstering her new
friend, as well, since this was Martha's first Christmas without her husband. Todd Moore had left his
wife and children for one of his students the previous spring; there'd been a certain amount of gossip
and speculation about it among faculty; even Tory,
who kept to herself, had heard it.

She set out for the town's police station. Becca
had asked her to bring the packages there for the
officers to deliver to the families on her list.

Amazing how much work the woman got done
while sitting home nursing a baby, Tory mused, trying to see around the packages and out her back

window as she changed lanes. A blue Jeep Cherokee was a couple of car lengths back, and in spite of the slow speed Tory was maintaining in an effort to prevent the packages from sliding, the Jeep didn't gain on her.

Tory switched lanes again. The Jeep followed her. She slowed some more.

The Jeep did, too.

Heart pounding, Tory took a deep breath and turned onto Main Street. The police station was left at the next intersection.

"Don't panic now," she warned herself. A lot of people in Shelter Valley drove slowly. The pace of life here was slow. She was just being paranoid.

Turning at the intersection, she refused to look in the rearview mirror. She was not going to give in to the panic. She was not going to do anything crazy.

She slowed as she signaled her turn into the parking lot of the police station, and pulled in carefully. With her eye on a parking spot, she concentrated on getting the Mustang into it. That was all. Parking her car.

Yet, somehow, in her peripheral vision, she caught sight of the blue Jeep as it drove by the parking lot, turned around and drove by again.

If those were Bruce's hired spies, they were getting bolder.

Tory stayed locked in her car for a full thirty minutes after the Jeep had left. It took her that long to stop shaking. And to convince herself the Jeep wasn't coming back.

This was the third time she'd thought she was being followed. If it didn't stop, she'd have to leave Shelter Valley. She knew the score.

Once she'd delivered the gifts, she didn't want to go home alone—to *be* home alone, a possible sitting duck. She drove back to Main Street, pulling into an empty spot outside Weber's department store. Big red plastic bows and glittering Santas adorned the street lamps along both sides of Main. Mostly, Tory ignored them. Holidays weren't for people like her.

But this year, the brightness of the decorations cheered her just a bit, left her feeling almost comforted.

She wandered down the street, looking in shop windows, but had nothing to buy. She'd already picked up several gifts for Phyllis and had no one else to buy for. She wasn't hungry, so the diner was out. At the end of Main stood the library, one of Shelter Valley's oldest buildings. With nowhere else to go, she ducked inside for a look around. Phyllis wasn't due home for another couple of hours. Tory could always lose herself in a book until then.

The interior of the library lived up to the building's promise. It was late-nineteenth-century, spacious, with marble floors, a display of framed historical photographs and solid wooden tables and chairs. Despite the appeal of its hushed and luxurious atmosphere, it was almost deserted; everyone was too busy being part of the Christmas hustle and bustle to have time for reading. Tory lost herself between ceiling-high rows of books, the solitude and quiet a welcome escape from her life.

She rambled through the stacks for more than twenty minutes, trying to choose a book to occupy these unexpected hours. It should probably be a critical study of American literature, something to help her prepare for the semester ahead.

Five minutes later, she settled on a couch in a deserted alcove at the back of the library, *Gone with the Wind* in her hand. Maybe not quite the studying she'd had in mind, but it *was* American.

And it suited her mood. Scarlet hadn't let anything stop her.

Tory's choice had absolutely nothing to do with the fact that it was a romance. Tory didn't believe in romance. Magic between a man and a woman was a tragic fantasy designed for the sole purpose of disillusioning young women. A rite of passage from carefree childhood into adult misery.

She turned the pages, hardly even aware that she was doing so. She was completely engrossed. Scarlet was fiery and beautiful and gloriously sure of herself. And Rhett—

"Mind if I share?"

Her mind filled with the breathtaking maleness that was Rhett Butler, Tory looked up from her book as someone sat next to her.

Her heart kicked up—in response to Rhett, she swore to herself, and for no other reason.

"No, I…" Her voice trailed off and she stared at Ben.

It wasn't as though his looks had changed in the two weeks since she'd seen him. Although minus the backpack she'd grown used to seeing slung over one broad shoulder, he was wearing his usual uniform of jeans and a short-sleeved shirt—brown this time. For some reason, the sight of Ben, relaxed and fit and tanned, was particularly attractive today.

Christmas might have come to Shelter Valley, but winter had not. They were still enjoying seventy-degree weather.

"You look good," he told her, seeming to approve of the belted overalls and knitted top she wore with her tennis shoes.

"Thanks." She stared back at her book, waiting for Rhett to sweep her away from Ben Sanders. Hard as she searched, Rhett was nowhere to be found.

"You enjoying your vacation?"

Tory nodded, leaning on the arm of the couch, as far from Ben as possible. Other than an elderly librarian way up at the front desk, they were alone.

"Have you heard anything from Alex?"

"No."

"Is she out of school for the holidays yet?" *Is there still someone keeping an eye on her?*

"Not until next week."

Tory glanced over at him—and then away from the warmth in his eyes.

"You still in contact with them?"

"Every day."

"Everything still all right?"

"Looks like it."

Tory sighed with relief, surprised by how much the burden of worry had been building during her time apart from Ben. She'd had no way to assure herself that little Alex was fine, that there was no reason to suffer for her.

Ben shifted on the couch and rested one ankle on the other knee. Tory's stomach fluttered when she realized he'd sat down without a book. Without even a magazine or the day's paper. As though he was sitting there solely because of her.

"Will you get to talk to her on Christmas Day?" she asked nervously.

"I doubt it."

Tory thought of all the packages she'd wrapped that week, the dolls and little-girl clothes, the games. Would Alex's parents make sure she had packages under the tree?

"Did you get her anything?"

"Yeah, I got her a stuffed version of Buddy." Ben grinned, though the expression faded quickly. "I picked up some clothes and a few other things, too, shipped it all off at the beginning of the week...." His gaze was unfocused.

"Your ex-wife will give her your gifts, won't she?"

"Sure," Ben said, glancing quickly at Tory. "Mary would never turn away something she didn't have to pay for. She just probably won't tell her they're from me."

"Who, then?" Tory asked, frowning as she

looked at him. "Surely she wouldn't pass them off as her own gifts."

"Of course she would," Ben said. And it wouldn't be one of the worst things she'd done, either. "But I don't really care as long as Al gets them."

"You don't want Alex to think you forgot her at Christmas, though."

Ben's brows were drawn together. "Unless it helps her adjust to her new life. Stop thinking about me and concentrate on her new father."

"Thinking that someone she's loved her whole life has forgotten her won't help, no matter how many new fathers she has."

"Maybe not."

Tory felt for him. There wasn't a whole lot he could do about the situation. To call Alex would displease her parents; there was a chance that displeasure would be directed her way, and if there was abuse in that home...

Face grim, Ben looked as though his thoughts might be traveling along the same path as hers.

"What, besides shopping, have you been doing with your vacation?" she asked in an attempt to distract him.

"Taking Buddy to obedience classes at the vet's." His grin was slow in coming, it was small, but it was there. "He hasn't quite figured out that he's supposed to be learning something—that it's not a social occasion."

"Is your friend Zack running the class?"

"No." Ben shook his head. A trace of the grin still tilted one corner of his mouth. Tory stared at that uplifted corner, finding it somehow endearing.

And then wondered what was the matter with her. *Endearing* was not a word that fit in Tory's life.

"Zack arranged the class," Ben was saying, "but if he taught it, the dogs would never learn obedience. He's too much of a softie. Lets them do anything they want."

Tory half smiled at the image of the big athletic man Ben had described being led around by a passel of puppies. Holding her place in the book with one finger, she said, "So, is Buddy a good student?"

Grinning fully now, Ben spent the next ten minutes regaling her with episodes from his week at dog school. She laughed as he described how Buddy sat when he was supposed to heel, lay down when he was supposed to sit. And lifted his leg on one of his fellow classmates. All in all, Ben thought his latest offspring showed potential. "Give him time," he said. "He's just new to being a Sanders. We'll retake the course in the spring. He'll get it eventually."

"I think you're nuts," Tory told him dryly, nervous again.

He'd made her laugh out loud.

Pulling her finger out of the book, Tory allowed it to close.

She supposed he'd leave now.

Looking down, she felt the cushion shift. Would he wish her a merry Christmas as he walked away?

Would he say goodbye? Would she ever see him again?

She sat there stiffly, expecting him to go, knowing she shouldn't *want* to see him again.

And knowing that she did.

CHAPTER FOURTEEN

THE CUSHION had shifted, but Ben was still on the couch.

What was he waiting for?

Tory looked over quickly and, surprised to see his arm along the back of the couch, almost touching her, she jumped. Her book fell onto the floor with a loud clap.

Embarrassed, uncomfortable, Tory bent to pick it up, but Ben got there before her. As she straightened, he held out the book, not releasing it immediately when she tried to take it. Unable to help herself, Tory met his eyes, the book a connection between them, her hand on one end, his on the other.

"You're not my teacher anymore," Ben whispered, holding her captive with the intensity of his gaze.

She never was his teacher.

He was going to touch her. Tory sat suspended, waiting. His hand was so close to her shoulder it would only take one slight movement. A split second. And then he'd be touching her.

Poised to run, filled with dread, yet unable to move, she felt trapped.

"I missed you this week." The words were soft, almost comforting.

Tory nodded, swallowed.

As though hypnotized, she let him continue to hold her gaze. His face came closer and still she stared into his eyes. He leaned so slowly toward her she could have escaped. If she'd been able to break that powerful eye contact. If her brain had told her legs to carry her away.

"Don't jump." The words were barely audible, but Tory heard them.

She didn't jump. She didn't move. She just sat there and let him crowd her, his face coming dangerously closer.

Until—frighteningly—she felt the softness of his lips on hers, hardly touching hers as he kissed her lightly. Nowhere else were their bodies touching. Just their lips. Eyes wide open, Tory sat very still, distantly aware that his lips were touching hers.

He pulled back just enough to break the contact, and then kissed her again, a little more fully, moving his lips on her startled mouth. She wasn't going to allow this. Tory hated to be kissed, hated what she saw as the male dominance inherent in the act, the suffocation.

"So sweet," Ben whispered, then bent to kiss her a third time. Not a hard demand, but a soft coaxing that confused Tory, until she closed her eyes, the better to think about it all.

He kissed her again, still touching her nowhere but her lips, and when his mouth left hers, Tory felt a little sad, a little cold. An instant later, he was kissing her again, and she was so relieved she kissed him back, her lips moving with his of their own accord, opening, tasting him.

Passion wasn't completely foreign to her, but it was so far in the past the force of it now completely surprised her. And possessed her. She forgot who she was, where she was. She knew only what she felt—and that the sweet power of it was stronger than she was.

He tasted like a man, yet not any kind of man she'd ever known. As she responded to him, the intensity of his kisses changed, full of mastery but still gentle.

She felt his tongue slowly travel the length of her lips before he slipped it between them. Tory moaned, pulling her tongue away, then slowly letting him find it, letting him pull her into the vortex of the sensations he was arousing.

Without warning, Ben's arm was wrapped around her. Exerting a slight pressure, he drew her toward him, sending a jolt through Tory that tore the air from her lungs and shot pure terror through her body.

"No!" she cried, shoving him away as she struggled to her feet.

She wasn't going to be trapped, held. She wasn't going to be confined by his greater male strength. She had to be free.

Free.

With only that thought in mind, Tory dropped her

book and fled. Through the empty aisles, her tennis shoes making plodding sounds on the marble tiles, past the astonished librarian and out the door.

If he tried to come after her, tried to catch her, she'd fight him. Elbow him, knee him, slap his face, stomp on his instep.

Tearing up Main Street, pulling her keys out of her pocket, Tory couldn't look behind her, couldn't give him the advantage of that small pause. Gasping and out of breath, she finally got close enough to her car to open the door, throw herself inside, lock the car. She'd kept herself safe from him.

She needn't have bothered.

He hadn't followed her.

WITH BETHANY SLEEPING at her breast, Becca Parsons stood in her kitchen, holding the phone to her ear with one shoulder as she dialed. She rocked slowly back and forth on her feet, the way Bethany had taught her. Becca had sent out more than fifty invitations to their annual Christmas party the week before, but had just that morning convinced Will to let her invite the two people she wanted there most of all. She had someone for Christine to meet. A bachelor brother-in-law of one of her friends. And someone for Ben to meet, as well.

Neither of them was home.

Afraid to take the chance that one or both of them might plan something else—though she was pretty sure Christine wouldn't, since Becca had it on good authority that Christine had no social life at all—she left messages on their answering machines.

"Ben, this is Becca Parsons. Will and I would love to have you come to our annual Christmas open house next Friday night. It's at seven at our home. Dress is festively casual—or casually festive. The Montfords are going to be here, and I'd be delighted to introduce you."

Hanging up the phone, she grabbed her folder with the specs for the new mine permit Shelter Valley Town Council would consider that evening and, baby still sleeping, stood at the counter riffling through the pages of figures. Although commerce was always important, Becca had a bad feeling about that mine. Given the land's history, it was very possible there *was* some gold to be found, but not enough to warrant the frenzy such a find would cause. No amount of money would be enough to justify that.

The issue wasn't a new one. Shelter Valley had been fighting the gold-rush craze since the discovery of the first mine, shortly after Samuel Montford had settled the area.

That first gold mine had brought the Smith family to town, and while they'd been influential in the town's history, they hadn't—not one of them—contributed anything out of the goodness of their hearts. Needless to say, Mayor Smith was the force behind this newest mining venture. But butting heads with their illustrious mayor was nothing new to Becca.

Neither was beating him.

The phone rang and Becca grabbed it quickly before the noise could disturb Bethany.

"Bec? Jamie just smiled at me!"

Becca grinned when she heard the joy in her younger sister's voice. She'd almost lost Sari to grief a couple of years before, when Sari's teenage daughter was killed by a drunk driver.

"She's only a few weeks old, Sar. It was just gas."

"No!" Sari insisted, and Becca could hear her pleasure, her unalloyed delight. "I *know* it was a real smile. I can tell."

"Bethany discovered her toes today." Becca had to do her own bit of sharing. "You should've seen her, lying on her back, staring at them, sort of surprised and trying to figure out what they were doing there. I told her, and I think she listened."

"Of course she listened," Sari said. "She's one smart little girl. Look at the family she comes from."

"Are you getting enough sleep?" Becca asked, still feeling a bit of leftover protectiveness where her closest sister was concerned.

"I've got the rest of my life to sleep," Sari told her. "Bob keeps saying he'll do the two-o'clock feeding, keeps nagging me to pump, but I can't bear to miss even one chance…"

"I know," Becca said. "But you might want to do it, anyway. You should see the look on Will's face when he's feeding Bethany."

For another few minutes, Sari expostulated on the

joys of breastfeeding, and as she listened, Becca was struck once again by her incredible good fortune. Amazing how life could turn around just when you thought it was hopeless.

"You ready for the party?" Sari asked.

"Almost. I wish I hadn't let Will talk me into having it catered. I miss doing the shopping and cooking."

"Like you have time to cook when you're taking care of a baby, tending to council business, running a toy drive. Something has to give."

"Okay, okay," Becca said, staring down at the map of the area slated for mining.

"I wonder what Mom's going to wear."

Becca didn't have to wonder. She ran her hand softly over her sleeping daughter's downy head. "Something outrageous, for sure."

"She'll probably hog the babies, too."

Probably. But Becca didn't care. She was just thrilled to finally have a baby for her zany mother to hog.

"DADDY?"

Listening to his messages, Ben came fully alert, head cocked toward the machine on his kitchen counter.

"I tried to call collect like you said, but you didn't answer and say okay, so I just called like you used to teach me…"

Alex's voice was thin, sounded unhappy. What

seven-year-old kid sounded that way on her Christmas vacation?

"I got spanked on my back again, Daddy. You told me to tell when it happened, and I got no one to say it to now 'cause I can't go to school. Anyway, no one's there 'cause of Christmas. Mommy won't make a tree. Bye, Daddy."

The sound of tears in her voice tore Ben apart.

"Ben, this is Becca Parsons...."

Ben paid no attention to his next messages. They didn't matter. Nothing mattered but making things right for Alex. One way or another, he was going to save his baby girl.

With the tenacity of a crazy man, he ferreted out the home number of Alex's school nurse, rang her house over and over until he finally got an answer, and wasted no time telling her the news.

"Of course the bastard would do it now," Ben said almost under his breath, not stopping long enough to give the nurse a chance to respond. "She's not in school, not under anyone's supervision. Beat her at Christmastime, and he figures he can't get caught."

"Yes, Mr. Sanders, he can," the nurse said quietly, with enough steel in her voice to get through even to Ben.

"So what are we going to do next?" he asked her, willing to take direction as long as there was a plan.

"*We* aren't going to do anything at the moment,"

she said just as firmly. "You're leaving this up to me and Child Welfare."

"You can't expect me to sit here and do nothing!"

"For now, yes, I do," she said. "We need you to be squeaky-clean, not cause trouble and interfere with the investigation. You have to be ready and waiting, Mr. Sanders. Alex will need somewhere to go if we do remove her from the home."

Pacing in his kitchen, Ben held the portable phone to his ear, hoping she'd say more.

She didn't.

"How long will you need?" he asked. A man could only take so much before he had to do something to help himself.

"I don't have that answer, Mr. Sanders," the nurse said. "I'll call Child Protective Services as soon as we hang up. They'll have to make a visit to the house, have Alex examined by a doctor, talk to her mother before we'll know anything more."

"You have my number," Ben said, and hung up the phone. Just a week before Christmas, and he'd never felt less like celebrating.

Buddy poked his nose into Ben's palm, asking for attention. As Ben squatted down automatically to pet the dog, his mind raced. He couldn't just leave Alex's call unacknowledged. Now more than ever, the child had to know she was loved. Desperately loved.

Grabbing the portable again, he dialed Mary's number, hoping Alex would pick up the phone. And hung up immediately when he heard his ex-wife answer. He could pretend to be selling something or doing a survey, but she'd recognize his voice in an instant. At least she wouldn't be able to figure out who'd called, even if she had caller ID. He'd requested an unlisted number when he moved to Shelter Valley.

"We could take a road trip," he told the dog, who was busy untying the lace of his tennis shoe. "Sit outside the house until I see a chance to get Alex alone."

And if he was caught, his chances of being squeaky-clean and out of trouble were nil. If he was caught, he'd lose his own credibility. The authorities might even be persuaded to believe the bastard was right—that Ben was just trying to make trouble for his ex-wife's new husband.

The dog jumped up, paws braced against Ben's stomach, and tried to lick his face. Lucky for Ben, Buddy's tongue wasn't that long.

"No kisses, Bud," he said in the uncompromising tone he'd learned at obedience school the previous week.

No kisses, Ben, he thought to himself, remembering the day before, in the library. He hadn't planned to kiss her. But it had felt so good. Like something inevitable, just waiting to happen. And she'd responded, no question about that. He'd been stunned when she started fighting him, and when she'd run off, he'd simply let her go.

And then he'd spent the entire night speculating about possible explanations for her actions.

Down on the floor, Buddy stared up at him.

"You think it was just a lack of desire for me, don't you?" he muttered to the dog. "You think I don't turn her on, but you're wrong." Buddy wagged his tail.

"Her reaction was too violent," Ben said aloud, although he was no longer looking at his dog.

Christine had secrets. Serious ones. And Ben couldn't rest easy until he knew more about them. Until he did everything possible to help her. Much as he'd like to believe he could walk away, Christine had become far too important to him. He'd been missing her like crazy since school had ended. Missing her, because he had no idea when he'd see her again.

And now he couldn't be sure, if he happened to run into her, that she'd even speak to him. Just when he'd been thinking he'd finally gotten through to her, that he could feel confident of her friendship.

And just when he needed her the most, needed to tell her about Alex, needed a second rational mind to depend on.

All in all, it had been one hell of a rotten couple of days.

"CAN WE TALK?"

"Of course." Phyllis put down the book she was reading and patted her bed. "You've had a rough weekend, huh?"

Sitting on the bottom corner of the still-made bed, one leg up, the other braced on the floor, Tory nodded. It was early Sunday evening, and Tory hadn't had an hour's peace since she'd run out on Ben Friday afternoon. She'd tried to handle this on her own. To escape back into that place deep inside where nothing touched her.

"I hope I haven't been keeping you up," she said. She'd tried to be quiet during her mostly sleepless nights—would've just left and opened up the Mustang on the empty Arizona roads if she hadn't still been jumpy from the encounter with the Jeep.

"You didn't." Phyllis fluffed the pillows propped behind her as she spoke. "But you've been even quieter than usual." She smiled gently. "And the shadows under your eyes were a bit of a giveaway."

Tory smiled back, although the gesture was without any real humor. "I'm losing my edge," she said. "Getting soft."

"And that's bad?"

Looking down at her hands against the soft cotton of her black sweatpants, rubbing one thumb against the other, Tory shrugged. "It is if I'm going to survive."

"Survive? As opposed to what? Live?"

Tory glanced up. "What's that supposed to mean?" she asked angrily.

"You've been *surviving* for years now, Tory. Isn't it time you started to *live?*"

Tory didn't know what to say. Her anger fled, but she had no response. She knew what Phyllis meant...and yet she didn't. Tory shook her head helplessly.

"What brought this on now?" Phyllis asked. Her legs were stretched out in front of her, crossed at the ankles.

"I don't know," Tory said, unable to tell Phyllis what she so desperately wanted to tell her. "This whole town, I guess. People talk to me when I go into a store. I know them."

"And that's bad?" Phyllis repeated her earlier question.

"No." And that was the problem. "Yes. It scares me."

"Why?"

Tory, meeting Phyllis's direct gaze, shrugged, not answering right away. "Because it's not real," she said at last. She spoke slowly, trying her best to release the furor inside. "*I'm* not real."

"Of course you're real, Tory! You're a living, breathing, *feeling* human being just like everyone else."

"You know what I'm talking about."

"Yes," Phyllis said, "but just because you have problems, difficult ones, doesn't mean you aren't as real and alive as the rest of us." Her hands, never still for long, gave emphasize to every word. "We all have problems of some sort."

Tory would have liked to accept that philosophy. "It's Christine they know and like, not me."

"*You're* the person they know. Only the job is Christine's."

But the job was a big part of the person they knew. The job earned their respect. Earned Ben's respect.

"I'm starting to care about them," she ventured quietly. "Becca and everything she accomplishes. I loved wrapping those presents, contributing something. And I like Martha. My students. Mr. Weber and his quaint little department store. The people at the diner."

"Yeah!" Phyllis leaned forward. "That's the best news yet, Tory. Don't you see? You're starting to heal. To be able to feel normal things. Shelter Valley is working its magic."

"And what happens to me when I have to run? How do I survive when I'm all alone again?"

Folding her legs beneath her, Phyllis continued to lean toward Tory. "The running is over."

Tory shivered, in spite of the sweatshirt she'd pulled on earlier when the sun had gone down.

"I think Bruce is having me watched."

Phyllis froze. "Why? Since when? Why didn't you tell me?"

"I'm not sure." Tory played with a string on the hem of her pants. "I keep thinking maybe I'm just being paranoid."

"It's possible." Phyllis nodded, but her voice was cautious. "Tell me about it."

Tory stumbled through the three occasions she'd thought she was being followed, ending with Friday's Jeep incident. She waited for Phyllis to calmly assure her that she was imagining things. That her fear was simply a normal, instinctive reaction to a life on the run.

"If it's Bruce's men, they must still think you're Christine," Phyllis said.

Tory's stomach knotted. "You think there's a chance I'm *not* imagining this?"

"Maybe," Phyllis said, her elbows on her knees. "What I do know is that we don't want to underestimate anything." The look in her eyes was dead serious. "We thought Bruce might keep an eye on Christine for a while. If he is, we'll just have to make sure that Christine is the person he sees."

"And how do we do that?"

"By doing exactly what we're doing. You've got a new life now, Tory, one you're settling into amazingly well. Everyone here believes you're Christine Evans. That alone should convince anyone who's spying on you—because people see what they expect to see."

"And what happens if Bruce comes here himself? What happens if he discovers it's me?"

Phyllis's gaze held Tory's for a long moment, and then dropped, her fingers clasped in front of her.

"Then I have to be able to survive running again," Tory said.

"He's not going to find you." Phyllis looked up. "His men are going to report the fact that Christine is an academic, just as she was in Boston, and he's going to be assured that everything is as he knows it to be."

That had been the plan from the beginning.

"You have a new life, Tory," Phyllis said urgently. "Don't let him ruin it, too."

Did she have a new life? Or was her time in Shelter Valley just another trap, like the one she'd been living in for years—sometimes safe but never free?

CHAPTER FIFTEEN

"YOU'VE MADE FRIENDS here in Shelter Valley, Tory. People who really care about you." Phyllis was still trying to persuade Tory, almost as though she could read her doubts.

But Tory was afraid to believe. Because she needed to so badly, and because believing would only make things that much harder if she had to leave.

"Who cares about me?"

"Becca and Will Parsons, for starters." Phyllis stretched out her legs, although she was still sitting forward. "There was a message for you from Becca yesterday. You're invited to the Parsonses' annual Christmas party, and of all the people in Shelter Valley, all the people Will knows at Montford, there are only about fifty on that list."

Tory tried not to let herself feel too good about that. "You're on it."

"Yeah, well, that's because I met Becca and Will at a very precarious time for all of us, and we kind of bonded. It stuck—like instant glue."

"Who else is going to be there?"

"Becca's family, of course. You've met Sari, and

she has two older sisters, Betty and Janice. Her mother, Rose, is a bit of a character. She lives in a world of her own, loves gossip, yet hardly knows what's going on, even in her own daughters' lives. And she always wears vintage getups, with flamboyant colors and these wild hats.''

Tory smiled. ''She sounds like fun.''

''Will's family will be there, too,'' Phyllis added. ''You might have met Randi. She's the women's athletic director at Montford, and Will's little sister.''

''I don't think I have.'' Tory shook her head. ''How old is she?''

''Thirty.''

Four years older than Tory and a ''little'' sister. ''She's married?''

Phyllis shook her head, frowning. ''Nope, and I can't figure it. She's a knockout, with short blond hair and the same big brown eyes that Will has. She's got a great sense of humor. She's fun. Terrific at her job.''

''Maybe she's not friendly,'' Tory said, envious of a woman she'd never met.

''She's one of the friendliest people I've ever known,'' Phyllis said, dispelling that hope. ''People just gravitate toward her. She's got lots of friends, male and female.''

''I'm looking forward to meeting her,'' Tory said. She propped her hands behind her on the mattress, leaning on them. Randi Parsons sounded intriguing, and if Tory could attend that party and just be herself, she'd probably enjoy her company.

"Martha will be there. She was Becca's maid of honor back when they were in college. And probably Will's friend, John Strickland. He's the architect doing the new signature classroom building at school. He lost his wife a couple of years ago, and I think Becca said he's spending the holidays with her and Will."

"Have I ever met him?" New people made Tory nervous. Bruce's spies were everywhere, could infiltrate any situation, as she well knew.

"No. He's not from Arizona, but he's been here a lot since last spring, when he first started working with Will."

Since last spring. Before Christine had even applied to Montford. He was okay then.

"Becca said she also invited Ben, because she's expecting the Montfords."

Ben. The subject Tory had been trying to avoid since Friday afternoon. The subject that had driven her to Phyllis's room tonight.

"He kissed me," she blurted out. Then cringed.

"He did!" Phyllis scrambled onto her knees. Smile fading, she asked, "Did you kiss him back?" Her voice was hesitant.

Tory nodded. Sort of. She licked her lips. Swallowed. Made herself go on. "I'm so confused I'm going crazy," she confessed, her gaze meeting Phyllis's.

"Because you like him?"

Tory shrugged. "I miss him a lot, I know that much."

"I understand."

Her hands back in her lap, Tory studied them.

"So did you like his kiss?" Phyllis's question was soft, coaxing—yet oddly respectful.

"At first, I was in shock," Tory admitted. "But he was so patient and gentle, and before I knew what was happening, I started to respond. I wanted him to keep right on kissing me." She paused, looked up at Phyllis. "I really felt honest-to-goodness desire, for a few seconds, anyway." She blinked, trying to dispel the tears that were gathering in her eyes.

"What happened?" Phyllis asked.

"He put his arms around me and I freaked."

Phyllis nodded, and Tory felt a little relieved. Her friend didn't seem shocked or disgusted...or despairing.

"Suddenly I felt trapped and I panicked. I shoved him away from me and ran like a bat out of hell. I didn't stop until I was safely locked in my car."

"How did he react to that?"

"I don't know. I haven't seen or talked to him since."

"When was this?"

"Friday afternoon."

"Have you told Ben anything about your past?"

Tory stared at Phyllis. "Of course not! We can't talk about that." And then she had a horrified thought. "You haven't told anyone, have you? Because if you do, Bruce is going to find out. I don't know how, but he will.''

"Relax," Phyllis said, placing a gentle hand on Tory's. "Of course I haven't said anything. I didn't mean to imply that you should tell Ben about Christine or any of that.''

"Then what—''

"I just wondered if you'd told him about your stepfather's abuse or your ex-husband's. Without mentioning names or divulging details.''

Shaking her head, Tory looked away, brought one knee up to her chin.

"Don't you think maybe you should?''

"No.''

"You care about the man, Tory.''

She glanced over, intending to deny Phyllis's statement, but meeting her eyes, she couldn't do it.

"And it's pretty obvious he cares about you, too.''

No. He didn't care. He couldn't. Tory felt suddenly chilled. And warmed at the same time.

"He needs to know enough about your past to understand that when you react like that, it's not *him* you're reacting to.''

"Why?'' What was the point? Tory wasn't living a real life, couldn't move toward a future based on the fallacy she and Phyllis had created.

"So you don't hurt him, for one thing,'' Phyllis said. More softly, she added, "and because he'll be able to help you, Tory. You care about him. You're attracted to him. This is your chance to heal.''

"I think Friday was proof that I'm incapable of normal male-female interaction."

And it was killing her. In spite of the fact that any feeling she might have for Ben could go nowhere, in spite of the fact that she might never be free to live a normal life, embark on a normal relationship, she needed to believe that, if the opportunity ever arose, she *could*.

"On the contrary," Phyllis said. "It proves exactly the opposite. You were with a man you care about. A man you trust and feel safe with, and because of that, you were able to feel desire. That's the best news we've had yet."

"But what about the rest of it?"

"It'll come with time, honey," Phyllis promised her. "With understanding and patience."

"I don't know..."

"Maybe Ben will have to adjust his technique at first, learn to touch you without confining you, but if he cares about you the way I suspect he does, he'll welcome the opportunity to do whatever it takes to help you through this."

It all sounded far too good to be true. Tory had a hard time believing such a person even existed. At least in her world.

"He probably doesn't want anything to do with me after what I did on Friday."

"He deserves to know why you reacted with such fear. You have to see that."

"What I see," Tory said passionately, "is that I have no right to start anything with anyone when I can't even tell him who I really am. You think Ben cares about me and...and maybe he does, but he doesn't even know my name!''

"Tory..."

"And I can't tell him," she continued, "because if I did I'd probably get all three of us killed."

ON MONDAY, Ben lost the battle with his self-control. Either he got himself some help or he was going to Alex. Who knew what could be happening to her while he sat safe and sound in his little apartment with his loyal sap of a dog, waiting.

We need you to be squeaky-clean... The nurse's words came back to him.

"Alex, honey, I'm trying," he said, startling Buddy out of his morning nap.

He *was* trying. But it wasn't working.

Grabbing his keys, Ben strode out to the truck. Alex needed him squeaky-clean. And he needed help if he was going to manage that.

He hadn't been back to Christine's house since Thanksgiving.

They'd added Christmas lights, red bows and a Santa with a sleigh to the picture-perfect yard.

Parking his truck out front, he paused long enough to wonder if he should be there. If, after last Friday, there was anything for him to find inside that house. He paused, but didn't stop.

There were some things he didn't understand about Christine, secrets she held close, but that didn't stop his strange compulsion to be near her.

There were some things that, while unspoken, were strangely understood.

He knocked. Rocked back on the heels of his casual leather shoes. Shoved his hands in the pockets of his jeans. Hunched his shoulders against the slight chill in the December air. He should probably have worn a sweater over his long-sleeved oxford shirt.

She wasn't home.

Or wasn't answering her door.

He knocked a second time.

He'd seen her car by the garage.

And then she was standing there, holding the door open in front of him, and all the things he'd planned to say disappeared from his mind.

"Ben?"

She didn't shut the door in his face. Didn't look annoyed to find him on her stoop.

She did, however, look confused. And uncomfortable.

And gorgeous in a pair of tight black sweats and a bulky waist-length sweater.

"Can I come in?" he asked.

"Sure." She stood back, allowed him to pass, awkward and stiff as she closed the door and led him into the living room. "Phyllis is at Becca's—" she said, and then stopped, almost as though she'd just realized that meant they were alone.

There was no mistaking the alarm in her eyes.

"I won't stay long," he was quick to assure her.

"No, that's fine. You can stay." She perched on the edge of the armchair adjacent to the couch where he sat. The smile she gave him was tentative, but completely sincere.

"He went after Alex again." He hadn't meant to say the words quite so baldly. But he couldn't keep his rage, his helplessness, contained a second longer. "I had a message from her on Saturday."

"Oh, God." Her face drained of all color. "No."

"She said she got spanked on her back again." Ben swallowed, forcing his clenched fists to stay by his sides. "The bastard's taking a belt to my baby's back."

Christine slid down to the floor. "I'm so sorry," she whispered, her face mirroring the pain he felt inside.

"I called the school nurse immediately," he continued. "They're working on things now."

"When will you hear from them again?"

"As soon as they know anything."

She nodded, her big blue eyes dark with anguish as she gazed up at him.

"She said Mary wouldn't make her a tree. The kid's seven years old and they won't even give her a Christmas tree."

"I'm sure that's the least of her worries at the moment," Christine said. "A tree would be almost a sacrilege at this point, a symbol of everything she doesn't have."

Ben watched her, his eyes narrowing. "You sound as though you know what you're talking about."

She started. Looked away. "I'm a teacher. We're trained to know these things."

She'd said something similar to him before. He'd accepted the explanation then….

"I'm amazed you're able to sit here so calmly," Christine said before he could follow that train of thought.

"Believe me, it's not easy," he said. "That's why I'm here, actually," he admitted. Arms on his knees, hands clasped, he studied the carpet. "They told me to stay put, not to do anything that could jeopardize my position. That way, they can get Alex to me if they find evidence of abuse."

She nodded. "I can see that. It's better for you to be here, removed from the situation. Because if you're there, it would be easier for your ex-wife and her husband to claim that your interference was part of the problem."

"Right. But in the meantime, I'm losing my mind. I think I've paced a permanent tread in the carpet at my apartment."

"What can I do to help?" Her voice was warm, sincere. Ben got lost in the compassion he read in her eyes.

"I don't know." He shrugged hopelessly. "I just knew I had to see you, talk to you. Being with you is the only thing I can think of that makes me feel better, calmer, more in control."

Though her eyes no longer mirrored her feelings, she continued to stare at him until tears started to gather in her eyes.

Looking down at her hands, she said, "Why is that?"

"I don't know." He paused, then dared to say, "I get the impression that you feel that way, too."

She was silent for long enough that he began to wish he hadn't said anything.

"I do." He barely heard the words. "Sometimes."

The tension inside Ben slid away, leaving behind a relief so profound he actually felt light-headed.

"I'm surprised you still feel you want to…be with me, after what I did on Friday."

Yeah. They needed to talk about that. And with all the time he had on his hands at the moment, why not now?

"I'm a little surprised myself," he told her.

"I'm sorry." Her head was still bent.

"I'm not sure you have any reason to be." A woman didn't act like that out of choice. She hadn't acted at all. She'd *reacted*.

"Of course I do!" She looked up. "I panicked and just left you sitting there. If nothing else, it was rude."

He waved her statement away, shaking his head. "I couldn't care less about that. What I'd like is to know why."

But he had a sick feeling he already knew. Her reaction to him—and to Alex's situation—were starting to meld into a scenario he didn't want to believe.

"I—" She broke off. Shook her head.

"You know what Alex is going through, don't you?" he asked, needing to help her just as he needed to know the truth.

Eyes down, she nodded.

Ben's stomach heaved. "Your stepfather?"

She lowered her head even more, exposing the vulnerable back of her neck to his view. She nodded again.

Every curse he'd ever heard spun through his mind. He just didn't get it. How could any human being look at a fragile child and act with violence? How could he not feel the instinctive need to cherish and protect?

He swore again, silently, when he saw the tears start to slide down Christine's cheeks. Ben was almost sorry her stepfather was already dead. He wanted to get his hands on the man's throat, squeeze the breath out of him slowly, painfully.

Except that wouldn't do a thing to heal Christine. But Ben had an idea what would.

If anything could.

"That's what Friday was all about, wasn't it?" he asked, dropping to the floor, facing her, his feet beside hers, but not touching.

She sniffled. Nodded.

"I felt so trapped I just lost it," she said, finally looking across at him. The despair he read in her eyes filled his stomach with rot.

"From the very beginning?" he asked, trying to

understand. He thought she'd been with him at first. Tentatively so, but with him.

"No." She shook her head. He was impressed with the courage it must have taken to hold his gaze. "I wanted you." She half smiled through her tears. "I really wanted you."

"You sound shocked." He grinned at her, trying, mostly for her sake, to make light of her declaration when, in truth, she'd touched him deeply.

"I am shocked," she admitted. "I haven't felt that way since I was about seventeen. And then, it wasn't nearly as...powerful."

"Age does that to a person."

She looked away then. "Maybe."

"For what it's worth, I really wanted you, too."

Her gaze skittered up to him and away, but he could tell she was pleased. At least a little.

"So what can I do to make the trapped feeling go away?" he asked softly.

Her blue eyes were on him again. "I don't know."

"When did the feeling start?"

"When you put your arm around me."

Odd though the conversation was, Ben was relieved they were having it. Almost as though he'd known without knowing that this was part of Christine's past. That caring about her meant dealing with her secrets.

Sick as he felt, he was strangely thankful that they were finally talking.

"He used to hold you down?" Ben asked, his jaw tight with the effort not to scream the words out.

She hesitated, and he knew she was still hiding some of it from him, but in the end she nodded.

She needed time. Space. He could give her as much of that as necessary. As long as she talked to him. Was honest with him.

"So we'll take things nice and slow." He chose his words carefully, trying to comfort, to reassure. "Find ways to touch that don't bother you. Not touch at all if that's what you need, until deep down you can trust me not to hurt you."

"You'd do that?" she whispered, tears in her eyes. "For me?"

"Of course I would."

"Why?"

"Because it's like I told you—being with you makes me feel better than anything I've felt before. Because when we first met, I felt as though I was finding an old friend. Because you're worth it."

"Oh."

He let her ponder that for a while. Pondered it himself. Where had his goals gone? His burning need to have a meaningful career before he allowed himself to care about anything else? Before he allowed himself to get involved....

Thinking about it, he realized he still wanted that career, but it wasn't what mattered most. Not when you looked at life as a whole.

"I intend to fight for full custody of Alex," he

told her eventually, breaking the silence that had fallen between them.

Watching him, Christine whispered, "I'll be praying you get it."

"I intend to do something else, too," he said. He wanted everything out in the open. There for her to deal with. Not fear.

"What's that?" She frowned.

"To ask you to marry me."

"Oh." She scrambled to her feet, wringing her hands. "I've just remembered I left some whites bleaching in the washer...."

"Christine."

She ignored him, was gone.

"Christine." Ben quickly followed her, slid past her to stand in front of her in the hallway, stopping her flight with nothing more than the space between them.

She held his gaze, but only for a second or two.

"I'm not asking right now," he told her, "and don't expect any kind of answer. I just want you to know I'm thinking about it. That I want *you* thinking about it."

She still didn't look up. With one finger under her chin, Ben lifted her head until he could look into those shadowed blue eyes. "Okay?"

She wanted to run. To hide. He could sense the impulse to do both. But instead, eventually, she nodded.

And Ben started to breathe again.

PLAYING IN HER ROOM, huddled over in the corner, Alex started to shake when she heard the knock on her door.

Last time there was a knock, it was Pete, and she got spanked. That was Saturday and this was only Tuesday, and sore places hadn't gone away yet.

Alex wouldn't tell Pete she loved him, because it would be a lie, and he already spanked her so much for telling lies. But he spanked her when she didn't lie, too. She needed to talk to Daddy about that, but when she'd called he wasn't there and she was scared to try too often because calling collect took so long.

"Alex?"

Mommy's voice sounded soft and sort of nice, not like it usually did.

"Yeah?"

"Can we come in, sweetie?"

Alex climbed onto her bed, hugging a teddy bear to her stomach. Her stomach hurt every day now and she needed to talk to Daddy about that, too.

The door opened slowly and her mommy came in.

"Hi, Alex."

"Hi." She was kind of happy to see who Mommy brought with her. The lady nurse from school. Alex liked her. Mostly the nurse just tested eyes, felt foreheads, took temperatures and called mommies. But she talked to Alex's daddy now and Daddy talked to her, and that made Alex like her a lot.

Maybe the nurse had come to tell her what Daddy wanted her to do.

"I'd like a couple of minutes alone with her," the nurse told Mommy.

Mommy had lines on her face like she wasn't happy. She stared at Alex, who held her breath. The nurse couldn't tell her about Daddy if Mommy stayed there.

"It's either here, or you bring her in," the nurse told Mommy, kind of mean, but she was smiling nicely at Alex.

Mommy nodded and started to say something to Alex. Her look said she was going to warn her not to be bad, but she didn't say it. Finally, when Alex's stomach was about ready to explode, Mommy left.

"How've you been?" the nurse asked quietly, coming in to sit beside Alex on the bed.

Alex scooted away a little and shrugged.

"Have you talked to my daddy?" she asked. "Did you come here to tell me what he says I should do?"

The nurse nodded and looked all sad and like something was wrong. Alex's stomach started to hurt worse.

"I've talked to him about your phone call on Saturday, and to some other important people, too. We all want to help you," she said. "But first, I need you to tell me what you told your daddy."

Alex didn't want to do that. Every time she told anything, she got hit on her back. And it was pretty much hurting all over. Last night in bed, when she'd rolled over and the teddy touched her back, it had made her cry.

And Daddy always told her to be his big girl and not cry.

"Your daddy wants you to tell me," the nurse said. Alex only believed her because Daddy had called the nurse when Alex didn't get to talk to him on Saturday. That made her stomach feel better.

As quickly as she could, she told the nurse about the man who lived with her and Mommy, and about Mommy not being like the mommies on TV, but that it used to be okay because Daddy was like the mommies on TV. And the daddies on TV, too. She told how Daddy was her best friend and that he was getting really smart at school so they could move away and be rich and never be unhappy again.

"Will you show me your back, sweetie?" The nurse asked when Alex was finally done.

Feeling bad just thinking about the spankings, and scared, Alex shook her head. Not until it was better. She was just waiting here in her room as much as she could until it got all better.

"Your Daddy needs you to help us out here, Alex," the nurse said. "We can't help you if you don't let me see it."

"It helps itself fine," Alex assured her. It just took some days.

"Please?"

The nurse looked like her teacher at school when they had important talks—about being kind to everyone and playing fair and not hitting.

"Why?"

"I need to see what Pete's doing to you, sweetie. It's called proof."

"What's proof do?"

"It gets you away from him so he can't hurt you anymore."

Alex studied her, not sure if that was really true. "Did Daddy say so?"

"Yes, sweetie, he did." The nurse smiled like the mommies on TV.

"Okay, but you better not tell Pete I showed you, and you have to be real careful," she said, turning around. "Sometimes my shirt sticks to parts, and it's not good for me to pull at it."

With her back to the nurse, Alex pulled up the bottom edge of her T-shirt with one hand, hugging Teddy to her stomach with the other.

The nurse breathed in once, fast and loud, right when Alex felt the cool air of the room on her back. "Oh, God," the nurse said, and then Alex's shirt dropped down.

She turned Alex around by the shoulders. "I'm so sorry, honey," she said. "So sorry."

"It's okay," Alex assured her. She didn't know why the lady had to be sorry. She didn't do anything. It didn't hurt when she looked. She'd been really soft with Alex's shirt, just like she'd told her.

"I've got papers that say I can take you and your mommy on a short drive with me. Would that be okay with you?" the nurse asked.

Alex didn't want to go anywhere. She wanted to

stay in her room. That was where Daddy told her to be and where he could find her.

"We'll call your Daddy when we get there," the nurse said. "He's waiting to hear from us."

"You promise?" Alex asked, hugging her teddy.

"Yes."

"Okay." Alex hopped off her bed. "I'm ready."

The nurse opened a big purse she'd carried in and left by the door. Alex hadn't even noticed it until now. She pulled out a big cloth bag and unfolded it. "Let's get some of your clothes and favorite things in here," she said, opening the bag wide to show Alex that it was empty.

Pretending she was going on a real vacation like some of her friends at school—only, instead of going to Disneyland, she was going to see Daddy—Alex did what the nurse said and put some of her clothes and toys in the big bag.

Then, taking the nurse's hand, she left her room.

CHAPTER SIXTEEN

ON TUESDAY AFTERNOON, Tory went to Phoenix with Phyllis and Martha to buy an outfit for Becca's Christmas party.

"You'd look great in this, Christine," Martha said, holding up a sleek black silk pantsuit. It was something Tory would choose—and something she couldn't have paid Christine to wear. What was it Phyllis had said about the people in Shelter Valley really knowing *her?*

Pleased, Tory took the hanger that Martha held up. "You really think so?"

"I'm sure of it. Don't you think this is perfect for Christine?" she asked as Phyllis came around the rack to join them.

Phyllis agreed, encouraging Tory to try it on.

Fifteen minutes later she left the store, the pantsuit in the bag she was carrying. She felt hopeful. If Martha knew her well enough to choose clothes for *her* and not Christine, was it possible that Ben knew her, too? Her, Tory, the person trapped in her sister's life? In spite of what he *didn't* know about her?

Later, while Martha was picking out a strapless bra to go with her new halter-top jumpsuit and Phyllis was returning an outfit she'd bought earlier in the year and never worn—an outfit that was now too big for her—Tory slipped away to make one more purchase.

A hardcover book. A facsimile edition of *The Last of the Mohicans*.

After a lifetime of reinforcement, she wasn't ready to believe in James Fenimore Cooper's hero, but she was a lot closer to believing in the man who did.

A man for whom she couldn't *not* buy a Christmas present.

But still, it meant nothing. It had to mean nothing. As long as Bruce wanted Tory, her life in Shelter Valley was nothing.

"PLEASE, HEAR ME OUT."

Ben sat with Christine in his truck early Tuesday evening. He'd told her he had something important to discuss with her. Something that couldn't wait. He'd left a message on her machine earlier in the afternoon and then waited by the phone, hoping she'd call him back.

She had.

He'd driven them out past the cactus jelly plant and into the desert, where there was nothing to interrupt them but the rattlesnakes and scorpions they couldn't see, the coyote they could hear in the distance. Cactus brush cast shadows all around them.

"I'm listening," she told him. She was practically hugging the passenger door of the truck.

I hugged the wall, Daddy. Alex's voice came back to him.

Ben turned, leaning against his door, facing her. As far from her as possible without actually getting out of the truck. "Relax. I promise I just want to talk."

"I know." She grinned, although it was still a little shaky.

She was such a contradiction. Strong and capable of fighting off whatever forces might haunt her, yet vulnerable as hell. Sitting there in her tight jeans and ribbed long-sleeved shirt that outlined her full breasts to the point of making him salivate, and yet sending don't-touch-me signals that a deaf man could hear.

He held up both wrists. "You can tie my hands to the steering wheel if you want."

He'd meant it as a joke. But her face was completely serious as she regarded him. "Do I need to?"

"I hope you know the answer to that."

"You could be warning me that you're thinking with your pants right now."

"I could be." Lord, if she knew how *much* he could be. "But I'm not."

"Then we'll forgo the idea of tying you to the steering wheel."

He was sure glad to hear that.

This wasn't how he'd envisioned their conversation. And his hopes hadn't been all that high to begin with.

Just yesterday, he'd promised her all the time in the world; he'd been able to give her a day.

"What was it you needed to talk to me about?" she asked, turning to look at him.

Taking a deep breath, trying to pretend that her eventual answer wasn't crucial to him, Ben regrouped. He steepled his fingers in front of him and gave her what he hoped was a reassuring look. He figured he might as well give it his best shot before things got any worse.

"I want you to marry me."

TORY SAT FROZEN. She might have said something, if she could think of something to say. If her throat wasn't locked, her lungs struggling to take in enough air.

She was still staring at him, but only because she couldn't seem to move. His eyes were brimming with so much warmth, she couldn't stay numb. But she tried.

"Before you answer, hear me out," he said, as though she might actually be getting ready to speak.

She continued to stare, wondering what more he could possibly have to say.

He wanted to marry her. He'd told her just the day before that she could have all the time she needed. He thought asking her to marry him now was giving her time?

Ben shifted his leg on the seat. He studied her, apparently choosing his words carefully.

He wanted to marry her. The thought terrified her. She'd tried marriage once.

He wanted to marry her.

And most devastating of all—the part of her that had survived kind of wanted to marry him, too.

"First, it would be a marriage in name only for as long as you need it to be."

What kind of fool did he think she was? "I won't be married to a man who takes his pleasure elsewhere," she said coldly.

Bruce, damn him, had taken her down that road, too. If she so much as talked to another man, he went ballistic, but she wasn't supposed to notice when *he* played with an occasional receptionist.

"Not only would I not do that to you, I'd never do it to myself," Ben told her. "I am a man of my word, no matter who I give it to."

Tory knew that about him. Her knees unclenched, her legs relaxing against the seat.

"I say that, not because I don't want to take you to bed right this instant, but because I won't do that until you're sure you want to be there."

"That might never happen."

"I think it will."

Tory would have smiled if she hadn't been so uncomfortable with the entire conversation. "You're sporting quite an ego there, my friend," she said.

"You really wanted me on Friday." He repeated her own words back to her. "Until I put my arms around you." He paused, the gentleman even then, giving her the opportunity to refute his statement.

But he knew she couldn't.

"So we'll make love armless for the rest of our lives, if that's what it takes."

Tory pictured that before she could stop herself. Ben lying on a bed, his arms behind his head. Her on top of him. Pleasuring herself.

Pleasuring him.

Whoa. She put the brakes on, staring out the windshield, rejecting the brief surge of excitement she'd felt. What Ben was offering might be available to someone else, to another person in another life. It wasn't something Tory could have.

She wasn't free. Might never be free.

She didn't know a lot about love, wasn't sure she could buy into that fantasy a second time. But one thing she did know: it wasn't love without trust. It couldn't be trust without honesty. And if Tory told Ben the truth, if she came back from the grave, they could both end up dead.

"Child Welfare has Alex."

His words cut through the tension between them. Obliterating it.

"When? How? What are they doing with her?"

"They picked her up today. They were going to send a social worker in, but the school nurse knew Alex would never trust a stranger and talked them into letting her go."

His next breath was more like a shudder, and Tory turned to face him. His face twisted with the effort it was taking him to maintain control when he said, "She took one look at Alex's back and moved her out. She said if there were any formalities to be followed, they could go in and clean them up later.''

It was more than a few superficial welts, Tory translated, sick to her stomach. She leaned forward, unable to tolerate the sensation of the door against her back. In a haze of remembered pain, she could feel her shirt chafing the tender skin of her back, making it sting.

''Where is she tonight?''

''They're keeping her overnight at the hospital and—''

Tory's sharp intake of breath cut him off. She couldn't even pretend to hide her horror. There must be a lot of damaged tissue, too many layers of skin gone—extreme danger of infection.

''She probably wouldn't have had to stay once they got her wounds salved and dressed and started her on antibiotics. They were able to bandage her up pretty well, but she refused to go anywhere else. She threw such a tantrum they figured it was in her best interests to let her stay right there.''

''For how long?'' Tory needed to swallow, but couldn't.

Ben shrugged. ''Maybe just till tomorrow.''

''Where will she go?''

Tory had visions of foster homes, strangers, people whose impermanence would frighten the little girl. Or worse. She didn't have a whole lot of faith in the system.

''I'm hoping with me.''

Her head swiveling toward him, Tory stared at

Ben. "Really?" she asked, a grin breaking across her lips. "But you're out of state."

"I also have visitation rights. The nurse thinks they can swing it to at least get her to me for Christmas vacation. From there, who knows?"

Tory's mind whirled. His face was mostly shadows in the moonlight, but she could still see his eyes. "The other day—when we talked—you told me you thought you wanted to marry me."

He nodded.

"So I know you're asking me because you really think you want to be married to me—correct?"

"Yeah."

"But the question came today because of Alex, didn't it?"

Suddenly the idea wasn't so threatening, so invasive. He really wasn't taking away her time. This had nothing to do with her needs or his; it had everything to do with Alex.

He nodded. "I understand if you can't consider the idea," he said, and though he sounded regretful, he also sounded resigned. "I don't want to pressure you into something you'll regret. But this afternoon, when I was speaking with people from Child Protective Services, the idea seemed so…right."

"You think that if you're married, you'll have a better chance of getting Alex permanently."

"I'm sure of it." He ran a hand through his curls, mussing them. "If I were her natural father, it wouldn't matter so much, but they're a little uncomfortable about turning a seven-year-old girl over to a man who is, in actuality, no relation to her at all.''

"But you raised her single-handedly!" Not that they'd care. Tory knew all about the vagaries of social services.

"Which is why they're giving her to me, why they're even willing to investigate the idea of permanent placement. Things would just slide through a lot more smoothly if I was married, could provide a mother for Alex.''

Tory wanted to help him. More than anything she wanted to help little Alex. Suddenly there was a reason for her life, something she could contribute to humanity. Who better to help the little girl through the months ahead, the slow frightening struggle to trust, the nightmares and sudden bouts of fear, than a woman who'd been there? A woman who was feeling her pain, caring about her, crying for her before she'd even met her?

A woman who cared about the little girl's father more than she'd ever cared about anyone in her entire life, with the exception of her dead sister.

"You haven't said no," Ben said eventually.

She still didn't say it. She didn't say anything.

She *couldn't* be considering this! There was no way she could marry him. Her emotional baggage aside, she was living a lie. If she did this, he'd be married to a dead woman.

"Are you angry?" he asked, leaning his head back against the window, one jean-clad leg resting against the gearshift, the other folded in front of him on the seat.

"No." The word was barely audible. Tory shook her head. She wasn't angry—not in the way he meant. Not with him. How could she be?

If she was angry at all, it was with the world, the life she'd been given, the choices that had been taken from her so long ago.

"*Are* you considering the idea?"

She tried again to say no, but the word wasn't audible at all this time.

Sitting forward, Ben turned, put his hands on the steering wheel, his feet on the floor beneath the dash. "I just want you to know that I meant what I said, Christine. You won't have to worry that a marriage license is going to change anything between us, physically, until you're ready. As far as I'm concerned, your battle is our battle. We fight it together."

Tears pricked her eyes and Tory fought them for all she was worth. She'd never met anyone like him. Wondered where he found the strength to be so unselfish. So giving.

Wondered if she could ever have that much strength. Or the courage to find out.

She stared out the windshield at the desert shadows around them.

"Say something."

"I don't know what to say."

"*No* is one option."

He was giving her a second chance. She still didn't say it.

"*Yes* is another."

Just thinking about that answer, about the possibility of saying yes, caused her physical pain. Because she wanted to...

"So you're considering the idea?"

In spite of how wrong it was, Tory nodded. "Yes," she whispered. *Yes, dammit, even knowing I'll never be able to marry you, I'm considering the idea.*

She'd done a lot of stupid things in her life, but this had to top the list.

"Thank you." She felt the quiet warmth of those words all the way to her toes.

She was a repulsive excuse for humanity, leading him on, allowing him to believe she might actually be able to help him. She had to tell him no. Right now.

But before she could say the word, she had a sudden flashback to a time fifteen years before. Her stepfather's face was red from drinking, contorted with rage. She could still feel the slap of his belt across her back when she turned away from that face.

Could feel the sheets sticking to her back when she awoke the next morning.

And she couldn't tell Ben no.

WITH SCHOOL OUT and no studying to occupy his hours, Ben found the waiting almost interminable.

He played several games of racquetball with Zack early on Wednesday, but by lunchtime his tension was so great he knew he had to get out of the apartment again. He'd heard from California Child Protective Services that morning. They were keeping Alex one more day for observation.

Tomorrow he might be permitted to go get her for the holidays. He'd know in the morning.

"Come on, Buddy, you need some exercise," he muttered after clearing away the crumbs on the counter from the bologna sandwich he'd made—and fed to the dog. He grabbed the leash, but before he left, with Buddy dancing and jumping around him like the good obedient dog he was, Ben called Christine.

She was on break, too. Maybe she'd enjoy a walk.

Walking was something they did well together. They'd had lots of practice at it during the school term.

Truth be known, Ben didn't really care whether they walked or not. He just needed to be with Christine. Her presence was a comfort he neither understood nor questioned.

THEY WALKED DOWNTOWN from Phyllis's house, where Ben had parked his truck, and then on to the park. It was almost deserted now, but it became a hub of activity during the summer, especially Shelter Valley's annual Fourth of July celebration. Both Tory and Ben had heard about it, and both said they were eager to participate in next year's festivities.

The previous year's celebration had included the dedication of his great-grandfather's statue. Ben wished he'd been there.

Buddy plodded ahead of them, pulling at his leash, his nose working overtime. Whenever he looked back to see what was keeping Ben, he seemed to be grinning.

"Phyllis said the Montfords are finally arriving back in town," Tory told him as they strolled through the park, enjoying the solitude. And the bright green, carefully manicured grass.

He'd been so consumed by Alex's situation that he'd forgotten the Montfords were supposed to be coming home. They weren't quite real to him, these people whose blood he shared. He was so used to being alone.

"They were expected sometime last week, weren't they?" he asked.

"Yeah, but I guess they ended up staying in France for a couple of days, visiting an old friend. It's not like they have kids or grandkids to come home to for the holidays."

There were many people who didn't have families to see during the holidays. They ought to get together and form some kind of club. Buy gifts. Have a big dinner with lots of chaos and people talking at once.

"They're coming to Becca's Christmas party."

Ben grunted. That was on Friday. A lifetime away. Anything beyond tomorrow morning—when he'd hear about Alex—was too far away to think about.

"Are you planning to go?" Christine asked.

She was wearing jeans again, tight ones, with a fleecy sleeveless red vest over a cream-colored sweater. Her sassy hair teased the neckline of the sweater, and Ben's fingers itched to brush aside those strands and touch the warm skin beneath.

"I guess it'll depend on Alex," he said. "I'm obviously not going to leave her alone, and I haven't been in a position to meet any baby-sitters recently."

"Martha Moore's got a couple of daughters who baby-sit."

"I don't know…"

"But it probably wouldn't be a good idea to leave her with a stranger so soon…" Christine put his thoughts into words—which should have surprised him, but didn't.

CHAPTER SEVENTEEN

BUDDY, GETTING TIRED, lagged beside them as they walked, his tongue hanging out. Christine glanced down at him and grinned.

"That has got to be the ugliest dog I've ever seen."

"Shh," Ben said quickly. "You'll hurt his feelings."

She laughed and Ben stopped. She was relaxed, almost happy. And was taking his breath away.

Buddy, meanwhile, sniffed the nearby six-foot-high hedge of desert bushes for an acceptable spot to do his business.

"Do you think Alex will like Shelter Valley?"

"I'm sure of it," Ben said, gazing around. He pictured Alex racing through the park, laughing and carefree, until the vision started to hurt. What if they wouldn't give her to him? What if Mary won again, convinced the authorities not to let Alex come home? What would happen to his little girl then?

"I just wish I knew for sure that I'm at least going to see her," Ben said, frustration brimming over. "I need to see for myself that she's okay."

"And you want to make sure she has a good

Christmas,'' Christine guessed. She was standing closer to him than she ever had before.

''A seven-year-old kid shouldn't have to remember a Christmas where no one would make her a tree.''

''Do you have one?''

Buddy sniffed some more, apparently in no hurry to move on.

''No, but if I get Alex, I will have.''

''Do you have any stuff to decorate it?''

He hadn't thought about that. ''No.'' And then, ''I don't suppose you'd help me pick some out?''

''I'd be glad to,'' she said, although she didn't look particularly glad.

''But we should probably wait and take Alex,'' she continued. ''It would be fun for her—and give her a sense of involvement.''

''Thank you,'' Ben said, gazing at the softness in Christine's big blue eyes. Her sensitivity touched him.

''You're right,'' he told her. ''It'll make a big difference to her if she feels this Christmas is really hers, that she belongs here, that she's not just a visitor.''

''We could go on Saturday....''

Buddy plopped down on Ben's foot, apparently planning to take a nap then and there.

''We could make a day of it,'' Ben said, warming to the idea, although he warned himself not to make too much of Christine's participation. ''There'll be a lot of crowds this close to Christmas, but we'll need sheets and little-girl stuff for the spare room in the apartment. Some games and books, too.''

''Might make good Christmas presents.''

''Sure,'' Ben agreed as the ideas kept tumbling forward. ''I'll rent some videos for her. She loves *Lassie*. And Buddy!'' The dog perked up one ear when he heard his name, but didn't lift his head from Ben's foot. ''She'll love Buddy. I can't wait to see the two of them together. She always wanted a dog, but there was no way I could take care of one back then, and Lord knows, Mary wasn't going to do it.''

''You really love her,'' Christine whispered, her amazement apparent.

''Of course I do. Don't sound so surprised.'' Didn't she know him well enough by now to at least take *that* for granted?

''It's just so new to me. A man caring for his child. First Will and now you.''

The admission was heart-wrenching, and Ben had to fight every instinct to pull her into his arms, cradle her there, give her the kindness she'd never known.

He put his hands in his pockets.

And stood, frozen, as Christine slowly moved her face toward him. Her lips were hesitant, hardly passionate, as they touched his. Yet he felt overwhelmed, thrilled, ecstatic. She'd kissed him of her own free will. Because she'd wanted to.

If Ben hadn't been so caught up in the sweetness

of her touch, the desire it was sending through him, he'd have laughed out loud.

Instead, under cover of the flowering hedge, he kissed her back. Again and again, his blood pressure rising with the intensity of her kisses. Until Buddy decided he'd rested long enough and wanted in on the fun. Yapping, he began to leap up.

For once, Ben was thankful for the nuisance. The dog had just saved him from trying to make love to Christine Evans in a public park and scaring her away for good.

"I THINK I MIGHT marry him," Tory told Phyllis later that night. The women were in the kitchen, enjoying cups of cappuccino before going to bed.

"Oh, Tory! Do you think…"

"Hold it." Tory stood, cup in hand. She helped herself to more whipped cream, took her time coming back to the table. "Just like everything else in my life, it won't be for real," she said before Phyllis could paint a picture that would be too excruciating for Tory to look at.

"And it won't be permanent." She sat back down, dipped her finger in the cream, watching it bob, white and foamy, on top of her coffee. Phyllis hadn't said a word.

"Just long enough for him to get custody of Alex."

As she finished, she finally dared glance at her friend. There was no sign of cheer on Phyllis's habitually cheerful face.

"Does he know that?"

"Not yet." Tory returned her attention to the whipped cream. "I haven't even told him I'll marry him."

"I'm assuming he's asked?"

Tory nodded.

Leaning her forearms on the table, Phyllis gave her a searching look. "Do you love him?"

An instinctive *no* on her lips, Tory stopped. "Define love."

"It's a combination of giving the other person your whole heart and trusting him completely."

Trust. A word so long absent from Tory's vocabulary she wasn't sure she even knew what it was.

"Are you afraid to be alone with him?" Phyllis asked, both hands framing her cup.

"No."

"If telling him about Christine wouldn't risk all our lives, would you tell him about her?"

"Of course."

"Do you think he'd ever deliberately hurt you?"

Tory was beginning to see where Phyllis was going with this, and she was a willing traveler on the journey, if for no other reason than to see what her destination might be. She suspected it was a place she'd never been before. "No."

"Do you believe the person he is when he's with you is the same person he is when he isn't with you?"

"Yes."

"Do you think he tells the truth?"

With curious fascination, Tory said, "I do."

Brows raised, Phyllis looked at her.

"I trust him," Tory said.

Phyllis continued to watch her, waiting.

"I do care about him—much more than I should."

Phyllis nodded. "You love him."

Tory couldn't make herself say that, couldn't travel any further with her friend. It was enough to know that she trusted Ben. Trusting a man was a new experience, an incredible thing in and of itself. Something she'd be thankful for the rest of her life.

"Are you going to tell him it's only temporary?" Phyllis asked, taking a sip from her nearly full cup.

"I don't think so," Tory said. "I'm afraid he wouldn't go through with it. And it would be pretty selfish of me to risk his chances of getting custody of that child just so I could clear my conscience."

"I suppose that makes some sense, but there's more, isn't there?"

Tory gave her friend a twisted grin. "You're too damn good," she said. "You're wasted in the classroom. You should be in private practice somewhere raking in the bucks."

"I love teaching," Phyllis said, her face still unusually serious. "And I'm not listening to you with my clinical brain. I'm listening as a friend, with my heart."

Unfamiliar feelings overwhelmed Tory—warmth, security, the knowledge she wasn't alone. All emotions that would become unbearable when she had to leave them behind.

"So why aren't you going to tell him it's temporary?"

Tory smeared melted cream on the rim of her cup. "Because he'll want to know why and I'm afraid I'll tell him."

"And we aren't wrong in thinking that's out of the question?"

Years of being on the run, of training herself to survive in hiding, had Tory shaking her head emphatically. "It's dangerous even for you to know," she said.

Phyllis smiled gently. "Didn't have much choice there, did you?"

Shaking her head, Tory went on, "You can never control what someone else is going to do with a piece of information. What if Ben thinks he can beat Bruce at his own game? It would be just like a man to feel he has to fix things. And...and how can I ask him to make a lifelong commitment to a dead woman?"

"Or, I suppose he could do what I almost did that day when I saw you guys sitting by the statue, and slip up. I was so sure that was Bruce, so upset he'd found you, I almost called you Tory."

Tory shrugged. "Every person who has that knowledge is one more chance that Bruce will find me. And the life of everyone who knows could be in danger."

Taking a sip of her coffee, Phyllis eyed Tory.

"There's always the chance that Bruce will move on now that he thinks you're dead. Find someone else to obsess over, marry her."

"Don't think I haven't thought of that," Tory said. "Hoped for it, dreamed about it. But I can't count on it."

"No." Phyllis shook her head, her red hair vibrant in the kitchen's bright light. "But if it happened, there'd be no reason for you to ever leave Ben."

Tory couldn't think about that possibility. Couldn't allow herself to hope. Or to worry. She could get through this, help Ben and his daughter, as long as she held steadfast to the idea that it wasn't permanent. If she started to think differently, to dream again, it would kill her.

She'd survived too many broken dreams in her life. She couldn't do it again.

"I wish you could at least go through the ceremony as yourself," Phyllis said, frowning again.

"If I did, Bruce would know within an hour."

"I don't know, Tory. I don't like it," Phyllis said. She pushed her cup aside, rested her elbows on the table.

"I don't, either." Not any part of it. "But I can feel that little girl's pain, Phyllis. I feel her physically, like it's all happening to me. I have to do this, to help her."

"And what about Ben? I'm assuming that since he asked you to marry him, he loves you."

Tory looked away. "He hasn't said."

"But you think he does, don't you?"

"He doesn't know *me*."

"Tory, you're just as aware as I am—"

"You said love included trust," Tory interrupted. "If I don't tell Ben the truth, he can't trust me."

"You've told him the truth about everything except the one thing you aren't free to talk about."

"It's a mighty big thing." Tory laughed, but there was no humor in the sound.

Phyllis reached her hand across the table, pulling back just before it touched Tory's. "There's no way you're going to make it through this without being hurt."

"I know."

But if she saved a little girl from the hell that was her life, if she could make Ben happy by giving him back the daughter he adored, if she could pretend, even for a week, that she was exactly who Ben thought she was, then all the pain would be worth it.

TORY WAS UP at dawn the next morning. She'd slept very little. If she was going to do this, she'd have to tell Ben immediately.

And she *was* going to do it. For once in her life, she would risk every ounce of strength she had to help someone else. Even if only this once, she would be the type of person she'd always wanted to be. The type of person she admired.

She was carrying Christine's name and she was damn well going to live up to it. She was going to put others before herself. She was going to have a reason to feel good about herself.

All that was left was to tell Ben. And she wanted to do that before he got his call from the social services people this morning. She wanted them to know that Alex would not only be coming home to her father, but that her father had provided her with a new mother, as well.

A respectable college professor who would bring only good, solid influences into the child's life.

BEN HAD JUST COME IN from a run with Buddy when the phone rang. Throwing the leash on the counter, he grabbed the mobile. He hadn't expected to hear from them so early.

"Sanders," he said, out of breath. And not from running. They'd better have good—

"Ben?"

It was Christine. He hadn't really expected to hear from her at all. He'd already mapped out his plan to stay in close contact with her.

"Hi there. This is a nice surprise," he told her.

"I just…the thing is, I've been up most of the night and…"

"Is everything okay?"

"Yes!" Her response was more nervous than affirmative, and Ben's muscles started to tense.

"I, uh, probably shouldn't do this over the phone, but I wanted to get it over with." He could hear her take a deep breath. "I wanted to speak with you as soon as possible in case—"

Hand to his forehead, Ben braced himself. "What's wrong?"

"Nothing. That is, I'm calling to tell you yes, I'll marry you."

The phone slipped down his sweaty palm and almost out of reach. He caught it before it fell. He sank onto the tile floor.

"Say something!" She laughed nervously. Not happily. Just nervously.

"You're sure?"

"I've made up my mind."

Which wasn't really the same thing at all. But he didn't think he could be noble enough to make an issue of it. All he needed was to get her married to him. Time, patience and love would take care of the rest.

"Well, I'll be damned!" He couldn't wipe the stupid grin off his face, not even when Buddy climbed onto his legs and tried to lick it off.

"Wait." Christine's voice held more warning than joy, but even that made little difference to the relief—the happiness—coursing through him. She was going to marry him. He'd have a lifetime to teach her about joy.

"I have some conditions."

Sure. Fine. Bring them on. As long as one of them wasn't that she planned to leave him. Anything else he could handle.

"You have to understand that I'm still not sure about a lot of things—"

"It's okay, Christine," he was quick to reassure

her. "I meant what I said. I won't pressure you into more than you're ready for."

"Believe it or not, I'm completely comfortable on that score," she said with a small laugh.

His blood started to heat. "Completely?"

"Yes, well, completely enough to trust that you meant what you said about giving me time."

That was actually better than he'd hoped. If he'd finally managed to earn Christine's trust, he was much further ahead than he'd realized.

"Thank you."

"You pack a pretty mean kiss," she said. Her words sounded thin, as though she couldn't believe she'd even said such a thing—and that earned her another piece of his heart.

"So do you, lady."

He waited, but she didn't continue the sexual banter.

"So, what are these conditions?" he asked.

"You have to understand that I'm only considering marriage at this point because of Alex."

"Just as the timing of my proposal was because of her."

"Right."

Ben pushed Buddy away, raised his knees and rested his elbows on top of them.

Whatever else she had to say, he was ready to handle. Christine had agreed to marry him.

"I can't promise you forever," she said softly.

Ben's leg fell to the ground.

"It's not that I don't want to…I think…but my

life is so out of control sometimes that I can't always trust myself, don't know how I'm going to react.''

Like running away from him in the library, he translated. It hadn't meant she didn't like him. Hadn't even meant she didn't like his kisses. She'd simply been unable to stop herself.

Okay. He'd known he was signing on for the long haul—long and maybe difficult—when he'd asked her to marry him. Knew, too, that every trial would be worth the effort if it meant he had Christine as his wife.

''Would you like to believe it's forever?'' He chose his words carefully. He didn't want to push her into a corner, but he had to know where he stood.

''Um, I...the thing is...''

''Just answer the question, Christine.''

''Yes.''

''Then that's enough for me.''

''There's more.''

He'd had a feeling there was.

''No talk of love, okay? Not right now.''

If that was what she needed. ''Okay.'' He could express his love without words. And hear hers, too.

''So, when do you want...I mean...''

''Would you be happy with a quiet, private ceremony?''

''Oh, yes,'' she said, her pleasure obvious. Ben wasn't sure it was too flattering to have his bride-to-be so delighted by the lack of formalities.

Unless the bride-to-be was Christine.

"Relatively soon?" He didn't want her to change her mind.

"How soon is that?"

"Next week."

"Christmas is on Monday."

"How does Tuesday sound?"

"Fine...I guess...yes, fine."

"Do you think Phyllis would like to be a witness?"

"Yes."

"Want to get together to make the arrangements?"

"Yes."

Standing, Ben grinned.

"I'm waiting for the call about Alex, and then I may have to drive to California to pick her up. Can I call you back as soon as I know what's happening?"

"Yes."

She sounded as shell-shocked as he felt. And yet, he didn't get the feeling she was trying too hard to run away from him.

"Okay. And, Christine?"

"Uh-huh?"

"I'm glad we're getting married."

"I'm glad, too."

They were the finest words Ben had ever heard.

CHAPTER EIGHTEEN

"DO WE HAVE to have a new mommy, Daddy?"

Alex, dressed in faded jeans and a button-up blouse, was sitting quietly on the floor, stroking an adoring Buddy. Mary had had Alex's blond hair cut short—for ease of care, he supposed—and it gave her an adorable elfin look.

Every time he looked at her, Ben felt a thrill of happiness, a surge of relief—and a sense of despair. His happy, vivacious little girl had done nothing more energetic than follow him around all morning.

He'd expected her to run him ragged with all the things she wanted to do. So far, they hadn't left the apartment. As eager as he was to show her Shelter Valley, introduce her to his new home—and, he hoped, hers—he'd been more determined to see her smile again.

She'd sobbed for half an hour when he'd finally been allowed to see her the day before. She'd apologized over and over as they'd shown him her back, told him how to care for the already healing flesh. She'd refused to believe she hadn't done something horribly wrong. And she'd refused, too, to let go of him, even after they left the office of Child Welfare.

She'd held his hand as he drove, until her weariness had taken over and she'd fallen asleep. Once they got home, she'd awoken only long enough to beg him to let her sleep in his bed. Just for that one night, he'd allowed her to do so. He'd been certain that once daylight arrived and she realized she was still with him, she'd be back to her precocious self. Ready to take on the world—or at least her new bedroom.

Now his heart wrenched when he saw the sad little face gazing up at him. He wondered if the fireball he'd known was gone for good. Ben joined her on the kitchen floor.

"Why don't you want a new mommy, honey?" he asked. They were due to pick up Christine in a little less than an hour. Both of them deciding to forgo the Parsons Christmas party, they planned to take Alex to get her tree, instead. Ben had put off meeting his aunt and uncle until sometime next week, after he'd gotten his new family settled.

"Because." Alex was looking down at Buddy.

"You'll love Christine, honey. She's pretty and nice and the sweetest woman you'll ever meet. She's a teacher at Daddy's school."

"Teachers are mean."

"Not all teachers. You liked Mrs. Dimple."

With her strict sense of fairness, Alex nodded.

"So why not give Christine a chance?"

Alex mumbled something, but all Ben caught was the last three words. "…just like Mommy."

"What?" he asked, running a finger along Alex's leg.

Not long ago, if his daughter was upset, she would have been in his lap, insisting that he hug her tight.

"Mommy said I'd like my new father, too. And he was...he was..."

"It's okay, Al, I know," Ben said when she screwed up her face in an effort not to cry.

"So, I got away from him and now you're doing the same thing."

It was a seven-year-old's logic, and it made a sad, twisted sort of sense.

He lifted her chin until she was looking at him. "Al, have I ever lied to you?"

With her chin still resting on his finger, she shook her head.

"I promise you that if you don't like Christine, I won't marry her, okay?"

The promise cost him, made his heart stop in his throat, but he refused to be intimidated. Al was going to love Christine. He could imagine nothing else.

"I don't like her."

"You haven't met her yet, honey. The deal's only good if you meet her first and really *try* to like her. Will you do that for me?"

"You promise not to make her my new mommy if I say no?"

"As long as you try your hardest to like her, I promise."

"Okay."

Her head dropped.

"I have a secret to tell you about Christine, honey," he said, running blind. And praying that Christine would forgive him.

"What?" Her face was lowered, her hand stroking the same inch of Buddy's fur she'd been working on for the past ten minutes.

Buddy, bless his mangy soul, remained still, allowing her to do with him as she would.

"When Christine was a little girl, probably younger than you, her mommy married a new daddy, too," he said, wondering if maybe he should've just kept his mouth shut.

But he'd always talked to Alex more like an adult than a child. She'd always seemed more comfortable with his honesty.

She continued to stare at Buddy, stroking that same inch of fur.

"He wasn't a nice daddy, either," he said, then stopped, but knew he had to finish. "She knows about hugging the wall, Al, and about...about being hit."

Her fingers stilled. Buddy lifted his head to discover the reason, then put his chin back on his paws.

"She wants to help you."

"Did she cry?" The tiny voice just about broke his heart.

"Yes."

A couple of tears dripped slowly off Alex's chin to land silently in Buddy's fur. The dog didn't object.

"When I told her about you getting spankings when you didn't do anything wrong, she started to cry again."

Without looking up, Alex crawled into his lap, wrapped her arms around his neck, buried her face in his chest and sobbed.

THEY WERE A LITTLE LATE picking up Christine, but Ben called, and Christine said to take their time. She offered to let them go alone to choose their Christmas tree, to give them another night alone. In spite of how badly he needed to see Christine himself, Ben was tempted to accept her offer.

Except that he honestly believed that Christine would be able to help Alex heal, far more than he could. She'd been there. She understood.

Alex waited in the truck when Ben pulled up in front of Phyllis's late Friday afternoon and ran up to the door to collect Christine. His daughter had belted herself into the middle seat and wasn't budging. He began to remind her of her promise, but thought better of it. Alex had had about as much as she could take.

The child was completely silent when Christine joined them. His fiancé wasn't all that talkative, either. Ben tried, at first, to keep a flow of chatter going between them, his eyes meeting Christine's over Alex's head.

He silently apologized for Alex's unfriendly behavior and begged her to be patient.

She told him—silently, as well, but quite emphatically—that there was nothing to apologize for. She told *him* to be patient.

He nodded. She knew far more about what was happening than he did. No more meaningless conversation. Hard as it was, he just drove and let Christine and his daughter do what they had to do all on their own.

Within ten minutes, and still without a word spoken between them, Alex had slipped her little hand inside Christine's.

THEY BOUGHT A TREE, a crooked, partially barren tree that Alex found on the back of the lot. She insisted they love it because no one else would. They bought decorations and lights and tinsel. And, sweating in the seventy-five-degree heat, Ben tied everything down in the back of his truck and took them home.

With Christmas carols playing and hot chocolate brewing, they decorated their tree. It was a quiet time and yet a healing time. Ben could feel peace settle in his small apartment and over the three of them and knew he'd made the right decision. All his life, he'd been the one girls ran to for help, a shoulder to cry on. And all of it had been in preparation for this time, this life, these two very special females who needed him.

Somehow he was going to be there for them. Somehow they would become a family.

TORY BELIEVED in the magic for five whole days. Through a busy weekend of making plans for their exchange of wedding vows and outfitting Alex's room with Winnie the Pooh sheets and comforter, with puzzles and coloring books and an entire set of Dr. Seuss stories. During a quiet, though fulfilling Christmas Day—Ben loved the book she'd bought him and didn't miss the significance behind the gift and Alex hugged her when she opened the Raggedy Ann doll Tory had bought her. The magic went on through Tuesday morning at the courthouse in Shelter Valley where, with only Phyllis, Alex and Zack Foster as guests, she and Ben were married. During those five days, Tory lived in her fairy-tale world.

His lips met hers gently at the conclusion of the short ceremony, and Tory wanted to cling to him forever. Wanted more of the sweet fire he sent through her body.

And then, Tuesday afternoon, they got home. Ben was unloading his truck from a trip to Phyllis's house, where he'd gathered up the boxes and suitcases Tory had packed with all her worldly possessions. And Tory was walking from room to room in the small apartment, looking at the two beds. One in Alex's room, and a queen-size one in Ben's. That was all. Nothing else.

Ben could have slept on the couch. Or she could have. If Alex's world hadn't needed to be so completely normal and secure and happy. How would they ever explain to the little girl that her daddy and her brand-new mommy didn't want to sleep in the same bed like all mommies and daddies who loved each other did?

And how was she going to climb into bed with her husband? Much as she wanted to, honest-to-goodness wanted to, she wasn't ready. She broke into a cold sweat just thinking about it.

She glanced in on Alex. Exhausted from the weekend, from the past months, the child was curled up with a stuffed Winnie the Pooh in the middle of her bed, fast asleep. Watching her, Tory knew she'd have to find the strength to go into Ben's room that night, shut the door and stay there.

Tory had never been good at staying.

Walking back into his room, she thought about the night ahead, visualizing Ben in there with her, the door shut—and started to shake.

But, astonishingly enough, not just from nerves. Her husband had a very attractive body. Made more so by his innate gentleness. His kisses raised feelings in her that she'd never felt before in her life— made her forget, sometimes, everything but him. What would it be like to do more than kiss him?

Would it resemble what she'd read about in books when she was a young teenager, still naive enough to dream? Would the feeling last through his possession, intensify, explode? Could the fairy tale really continue?

Ben came in, and she turned nervously, an embarrassed smile on her face.

He wasn't smiling.

In fact, she'd never seen that look on his face before. A mixture of shock, bitterness and anger.

"What's wrong? What happened?" she asked. He must have received word about Alex.

"Explain that."

Tory's stricken gaze fell on the little blue book he dropped on the dresser. Christine's bank book. From the account that was really Tory's. It was her escape account. The one she'd been secretly filling for years. The one Christine administered because Bruce had never found her sister enough of a threat to investigate.

Inside that book was a bank card to access the account. A bank card with Christine's picture on it.

Feeling the blood drain from her entire body, Tory couldn't pick up that incriminating little plastic book.

"Your file case fell off the end of the truck," Ben explained, his voice emotionless. "Either you didn't have it locked or the lock wasn't worth a damn."

She'd been having troubles with the lock. But living in Shelter Valley, with Phyllis, she'd gotten soft, hadn't been as careful. And she should have been. Bruce's hired snoops could just as easily have found that book. They could have broken into Phyllis's house without their even knowing and found out anything Bruce needed to know.

A lock wouldn't have stopped them. And they would have learned the shocking truth.

Smart though Bruce had been, he'd made one mistake over the years. He'd never seen Christine's strength, her iron will. He'd only ever seen a beaten woman, one he could terrify with only a glance. He'd never searched her house or her things. The most he'd ever done was have her phone tapped for contacts with Tory when Tory ran. And watched her mail for letters.

"Who are you?" Ben's harsh words brought her back to the present with a crash.

"Tory. Tory Evans."

If it was possible for an emotionless face to grow even more numb, Ben's did. Almost as though, until that moment, he'd still been hoping she wouldn't destroy his faith in her.

"Christine's sister?"

He had a good memory. Tory swallowed. Nodded.

"Where is Christine?"

"Cremated in New Mexico."

He sat down hard on the end of the bed. Aware of Alex in the other room, Tory shut the bedroom door, leaning against it.

"So that much was true."

It seemed so long ago since she'd told him about the car accident. Tory nodded again, and when she realized he couldn't see her response since he was looking everywhere but at her, she said, "Yes." Her voice cracked.

His eyes raked her up and down, making her feel naked even in her jeans and sweater. She shivered.

"How old are you?"

That was a question she could answer. Which

meant she'd have at least another second before he asked one she could not. "Twenty-six."

"Hardly old enough to have your doctorate," he said. Knowing her silence was going to incriminate her, Tory still didn't say a word. Besides, she couldn't think of anything to say that would make a difference.

With a dread she couldn't prevent, she saw realization dawn.

"You don't have a doctorate."

She shook her head.

"Do you have any degrees at all?"

Again, a quick shake of the head.

"It's all a lie, isn't it?" he asked, standing. He shoved his hands in his pockets, strode to the window and turned to face her again. "You aren't an English teacher. The degrees are your sister's, not yours—you didn't just steal her name. For some sick reason, you stole her entire identity."

Eyes filled with contempt, he stared her down. Tory nodded.

"You *married* me under an assumed identity."

She could see all the truths slamming into him at once, and hated herself all over again.

She'd been so very, very careful. Who could ever have guessed that her file would be the one thing to fall out of his truck? And that the lock would choose that moment to give? But if this hadn't happened, there would've been something else. She'd attempted the impossible. There were just too many ways Ben could have figured out that she wasn't who she'd claimed to be. Like when school started again and she had to start cramming like crazy to learn her stuff.

She'd known she was living on borrowed time.

"I'm married to a dead woman!"

She'd known it was coming. Wringing her hands, Tory stood there with absolutely no idea what to do. Her experiences with conflict had involved either physical pain—or running.

But Ben was never going to beat her. And she couldn't run from him.

Phyllis would be thrilled.

Ben ran his fingers through his hair, mussing it further, then shoved his hand back in his pocket.

"Why?"

Licking her lips, Tory took a deep breath. "I can't tell you."

"You'd damn well better tell me."

With Bruce she would have cringed, waiting for the blow. But with Ben, she didn't. He wasn't going to hit her. He'd probably throw her out. He would almost certainly break her heart. But he wasn't going to hit her.

Tory almost wished he would. *That* she knew how to deal with.

"I can't believe it happened again," he said, pacing the room. "First Mary and now you."

"What?"

For all her faults, Tory was nothing like his ex-wife. Tory cared. About him. About Alex.

"At least she didn't lie about who she was," he

said, almost to himself. "No, she just lied to me about who Alex is. But you—" he turned, coming closer "—you lie to me about your very existence." Turning back before he reached her, he said again, "I can't believe this. I'm married to a dead woman."

Tory stood there, tears gathering in her throat, behind her eyes, as she listened to the anguish in his voice. She'd done this for him. Married Ben to help him get the one thing he wanted most in the world. She'd done this for Alex.

And had still ended up causing pain.

"You have to tell me why," he said fiercely, turning back toward her.

Tory shook her head. "I can't," she whispered through her tears. "Can't you please believe that I would if I could?"

Phyllis had told her that the people in Shelter Valley knew *her*, Tory, that they cared about her. That Christine was only an exterior.

"Can't you please trust me?" she begged.

"Trust you?" Ben reached for the doorknob, waiting for Tory to move before he pulled open the door. "That's rich," he said. "Until ten minutes ago, I didn't even know your name. How the hell can you expect me to trust you?"

With one last disgusted—and disillusioned— glance at her, he left, his last words ringing in her ears.

How could she expect him to trust her?

She didn't.

The fairy tale had ended.

TORY DIDN'T SEE him again until just before dinnertime. He came to find her in the bedroom, which, she now presumed, they were not going to share. She'd left all her stuff packed, waiting to find out what he wanted her to do. How he wanted to explain things to Alex.

He didn't intend to explain anything to Alex, he told her. He figured, after all she'd done, she owed it to him to play the role a little while longer. At least through the holidays, until he knew more about Alex's future.

Obviously prepared for a fight, he spit out one demand after another.

She was to pretend she loved him, do things with him and Alex, and put up with sleeping in his bed. She didn't have to worry, he told her bluntly; he had no desire to be there, no desire to touch her. He just wanted his little girl to think she had a normal life. Even if only for a few days.

In other words, Tory was expected to continue with the marriage as though none of this had happened.

She agreed—on one condition. That he allow her Christine charade to continue.

THE LAST WEEK of December might not have been cold in Shelter Valley, but you wouldn't know it by Ben's heart. He felt as though a very big part of him had turned to ice. The things Mary had done to him were child's play in comparison to finding out that the woman he adored didn't even exist.

Except that, as the days passed, as he saw Tory with Alex, witnessed the magic she worked so patiently, so gently, with his little girl, he began to recognize the woman who'd completely filled his thoughts these past few months.

Just as she went above and beyond with her students at the university, so she tended to him and Alex at home. No matter how grouchy he got with her, she quietly accepted whatever he had to say. She cleaned up after Buddy without complaint.

She was smart, savvy and, he sometimes thought, stronger than he was.

The only time she fought Ben was when it came to Alex. She was very protective of the little girl and wouldn't let Ben do or say anything that had the slightest chance of affecting Alex adversely.

Like the time he'd tried to keep Alex out of their bedroom, thinking it best that she sleep in her own room, because routine and normalcy were important.

That night Alex slept between the two of them. And the next night was back in her own bed, just as she'd promised Tory. Tory had let the child know they were there for her when she really needed them. And when she didn't, they were right across the hall.

Other things weren't going quite as he'd planned, either. He'd expected that he'd never want to touch his lying wife again. But night after night, as he lay in bed beside her, smelled her fresh, feminine scent, he found it harder and harder not to reach for her. Not to lean over and kiss that vulnerable spot at the back of her neck. Not to accidentally let his foot slide over and rub against her leg.

He sure as hell couldn't blame his reaction on any encouragement or teasing on her part. She wore sweats and a T-shirt to sleep in and hung half out of bed in an attempt to keep to her side.

"What are you going to do when the semester starts?" he asked her as they were preparing dinner a few days after they were married.

With new understanding, he thought back to the times she'd lacked self-confidence, in spite of her thorough mastery of the material she'd been teaching.

She looked up from the macaroni-and-cheese she was stirring. "Teach."

"But—"

"Christine's a teacher. I have to teach," she said in the same tone she'd used in the classroom when she'd been absolutely certain of something.

Ben let it go, but he wasn't satisfied.

He'd never been so confused in his life. The woman he'd known these past months, the woman he'd grown to care so much about, was now living in his house, sleeping in his bed. He could no longer deny that.

He just didn't know who she was.

Or why she'd engaged in such a massive deception.

He also didn't know how she'd come to know so much when she had no formal education.

But he *wanted* answers to all these questions.

Two days before the year ended, Ben entered his apartment after taking Alex over to play with Martha Moore's youngest daughter. He found Tory sitting on the edge of the living-room couch, her face ashen, tears streaming down her cheeks, an unfolded piece of paper clasped between her fingers.

''Tory?'' he asked. He'd gotten used to the name. He actually thought it suited her better than the more conventional Christine, but honoring her request, he only used it when they were alone.

She looked up at him, helpless as a child, her mouth moving but no words coming out.

''What is it?'' he asked. Alarm filled his heart, propelling him over to her. If someone had hurt her, he'd—

''He's dead,'' she said, her voice devoid of emotion, in spite of the tears.

''Who's dead?''

''Bruce,'' she said, as though they'd just been talking about him, as though they'd frequently spoken about him. ''Bruce is dead.''

Who was Bruce? What did he mean to Tory?

''He killed himself. One of his servants, who'd been a bit of a friend to me, wrote to Christine, telling her about Bruce's death.''

She sounded dazed, as though she still couldn't comprehend that this man—whoever he was—had died.

Confused, Ben sat down next to her. ''I'm sorry,'' he said.

"Oh, no!" She swung her head toward him, her teary eyes earnest. "Don't be sorry, *please* don't be sorry. This is the best news I've ever had!"

Even more worried now, Ben watched her. Had she completely flipped out? Should he call Phyllis? Get her to a hospital?

Before he could reach for the phone, Tory grabbed his hand. "I'm free, Ben! Really and truly free!"

He was missing something vitally important here. Something he desperately needed to know.

Something he was about to find out.

"All the years of running, the fear, the beatings. It's all over!" She stared at him, her face a mixture of disbelief and innocence. "I can't believe it. It's f-finally over."

She burst into tears, falling against Ben's chest, clutching his shoulders much like Alex had done when he'd brought her home from Child Welfare. Ben's body shook with the force of Tory's sobs. His heart ached with the force of her pain.

Careful not to confine her in his embrace, he nonetheless held her, one hand on her thigh, the other gently rubbing her arm. Held her and rode out the storm with her. He had no idea what she was seeing in the shadows he couldn't see, what pain she was releasing. He knew only that this was the woman he loved.

No matter what she called herself.

When she was breathing more regularly, he started to talk.

"Tell me about him," he said, bracing himself for whatever might come next. He knew that whoever Bruce might be, he wasn't the stepfather who'd abused her. That despicable excuse for a human being had died several years ago.

"He wouldn't let me go to college," she said. "I wanted so badly to follow in Christine's footsteps, to make something of myself, to get out..."

She began to shudder, to weep silently, and she was lost to him again.

"Why wouldn't he let you go?" Ben asked, calling her back. *And what right did he have to stop you?*

"He was jealous, thought I'd fool around with the college boys." She was quiet for a moment, then added, "And I think he was afraid to let me get an education in case it made me too independent."

Nausea hit Ben's stomach. "Who was he, Tory?"

"My ex-husband."

Emotions attacked Ben from all angles during the next hour as he sat and listened to the horror of Tory's marriage, the more than two years of running since. Compassion, protectiveness, overwhelming love mingled with rage, despair, helplessness.

And gratitude. He was so thankful that she'd found Phyllis. And that because of their daring plan, *he'd* found Tory.

"I don't know why it is that girls who've been abused as children often pick abusive men for husbands, but Phyllis says it's a common pattern," she said at one point. "It's almost like I expected him to hurt me. And Bruce, of course, obliged."

Right then, if Bruce hadn't already been dead, Ben could cheerfully have murdered the man with his own bare hands.

"It's a pattern you've broken this time," he assured her instead.

She nodded, her head moving against his chest. "I know that."

Her hand dropped to his, where it rested on her thigh. His breath caught as she slipped her fingers beneath his. He'd watched her hold Alex's hand many times over the past few days. This was the first time she'd ever held his.

"I wanted so badly to tell you—"

"Shh." He placed the fingers of his free hand against her lips. "I understand that now. One slip, and Bruce could have been on to you. On to all of us. And there's no guarantee I wouldn't have gone after him, either."

The way he felt, chances were actually pretty good that he'd have tried to play the superhero. And could easily have gotten them all killed.

"I really was thinking of you and Alex when I agreed to marry you," she told him, though she didn't need to. He'd already figured that out himself. "And protecting you with my silence."

"It's over, Tory." At least, that part of it was. Much remained to be seen.

"He used to force me to have sex with him, and the whole time he'd tell me how much I was liking it, how much I wanted it. But I hated it. I was certain I'd never want sex again—until I met you.''

Sitting there so close to her, closer then she'd ever allowed, Ben was deeply touched by her admission. He had a legacy of hurt to overcome, but he was determined to do so—as long as she'd let him.

He wasn't sure how much damage he'd done over the past few days. Tory's emotional trust was so fragile his rejection could have been enough to destroy it.

''He used to make me throw these huge parties, and everything had to be perfect from my clothes to the music. And if any of the food wasn't eaten or the wine wasn't the best, I'd pay later. He'd say I didn't really want to be his wife, didn't really love him if I didn't do better than that....''

Holding his hand, Tory continued to talk. And Ben listened, all the while struggling to keep his emotions in check. There was nothing he could do, no way to wipe away the memories haunting her, the pain she'd endured. Yet he felt an instinctive need to do something.

''So what finally made the bastard snap?'' Ben asked a little later, as her narrative slowed to a few random memories.

''He'd been having me watched—me as Christine....''

Ben's heart turned to ice when she told him about the times she'd been certain she was being followed, right here in Shelter Valley, as recently as the Friday before she'd agreed to marry him. The day he'd first mentioned marriage to her.

"When his men reported back that 'Christine' had spent an entire semester teaching college, told him about the life she was living, the man she was seeing, he finally became convinced I was dead," Tory told him. "I would never have been openly seen with another man. He'd have killed me, and he knew that I knew it." She held out the page she'd been reading. "According to this letter, he was so distraught, so unwilling to face life without me, he hanged himself so he could join me, instead."

Ben needed to hug her so badly, and knew she needed just as badly *not* to be hugged.

Someday, he vowed. Someday.

No matter how long it took.

But first he had some making up to do.

"I'm so sorry I've been such an idiot," he told her, sparing himself nothing. "You've been so good to me, so great with Alex, and I couldn't even say thank-you."

"I wasn't doing it for gratitude."

"I know."

"And I think you were very gracious toward me, under the circumstances," she added, pulling her head back enough to smile up at him. "I don't think *I'd* have been that gracious if I'd just found I'd married a dead man…"

"We're going to have to take care of that."

"I know. I intend to call Will first thing in the morning. I could be in some real trouble there."

"Maybe." Ben refused to think about that. Tory had had enough trouble in her life. Now was the time for her payoff. "But Will's a good man. If we explain the circumstances, I'm pretty sure he won't press charges against you."

"It'll take a little longer with the authorities. I don't even know how to go about proving they issued a death certificate for the wrong woman."

"I'm not sure of procedures, either, but whatever they are, we'll get through them."

"We?"

Ben took a deep breath, prayed he'd get this right. "I didn't marry a teacher, Tory, or a thirty-year-old. I married the woman whose soul spoke to mine the first day I met her, whose presence can calm me even when my world in falling apart. One who's intelligent, who has courage and strength and compassion. A woman who loves my little girl, who's bringing the sparkle back to Alex's eyes..."

She was crying softly. "I don't deserve you," she whispered. "Mostly, I can't even believe you're real."

"I'm very real, my darling," he assured her. "Someday, when you're ready, I'll show you how real."

A small movement against him was her only re-action to his promise. "Does this mean you want to stay married to me?"

"It means I intend to marry you again—and get the name right this time. That is, if you agree."

"I agree," Tory said without hesitation. She

smiled at him, leaning forward to place a small, provocatively innocent kiss on the corner of his mouth.

"I'll make the calls tomorrow morning," he said. He wanted to be legally married to this woman as soon as he could possibly arrange it.

Just as he mentioned the telephone, it rang on the table beside her. Picking up the receiver, she handed it to Ben and then watched, her eyes intent, as he heard the news he'd been waiting for.

"We've got Alex!" he shouted a few minutes later when he hung up the phone.

"It's official?"

"It's official temporarily," he said, so relieved he wanted to run a mile. "There'll be a lot of paperwork, some visits from a social worker, a court hearing or two, depending on how difficult Mary tries to be."

"If she knows what's good for her, she's not going to fight. Or she and Pete could very well end up in jail."

"I'm certainly in favor of that, although the only thing I really care about is getting Alex." He grinned and grabbed his wife's hands. "In the meantime, I'm to enroll her in school here in Shelter Valley."

"Thank God."

"We're going to be a family, Tory—you, me and Alex."

Tory sighed, a residual sob making her breath uneven. "I still can't figure out why you'd want to saddle yourself with someone like me."

Ben kissed the top of her head. "Life isn't really about creating our own fates or even choosing them. It's about making of them what we can, to the best of our ability." He kissed her lightly. "And we're both examples of that."

"Ben?"

"Yeah?"

"I think I'd like to make love with you, to the best of my ability...."

Fortunately, Alex was at Martha's house for another couple of hours.

* * * * *

*Turn the page to read the
beginning of Tara Taylor Quinn's
next* SHELTER VALLEY *story,
WHITE PICKET FENCES.*

*WHITE PICKET FENCES
is available next month,
wherever Harlequin books are sold.*

*Join your friends in Shelter Valley,
and read about Randi Parsons
as she, too, finds the love
she's looking for—with
the last man she expects!*

CHAPTER ONE

SOMETHING WAS MISSING.

Trailing through her house, leaving lights on in her wake, Randi Parsons frowned. Why did she have this odd, empty feeling?

She'd painted and tiled her little living room last summer. She'd bought a luscious daybed ensemble with matching everything for her spare bedroom over Thanksgiving. And now, during Christmas break, she'd given the kitchen a coat of yellow paint, papered the small wall in the breakfast alcove with wild flowers and hung curtains.

Her little house was finally as she'd envisioned it when she'd bought it eighteen months before. She should feel satisfied. Complete.

Making her way into the master bedroom, she scrutinized it carefully for anything amiss. The maroons in her comforter and pillow shams, the plush towels in the bathroom and the undertones in the handwoven tapestry rug on the bathroom floor were all as they should be. Just as she wanted them.

She loved this room.

So what was missing?

It was Tuesday morning, the second of January.

She had another week before she had to report back to school, once again taking up her position as Athletic Director at the university. Though she'd been hoping to make it to Phoenix for several rounds of golf with some friends, her living space was important. She could do more here if she needed to. But what?

Finding no answers inside the house, Randi wandered outside. Shelter Valley's blue skies and sunshine she took for granted, though she loved them, too. Even the 65 degree temperature was a given. The tiny patch of grass in her front yard was as green and verdant as it should be. The stucco finish on the house looked great.

Sitting on the boulder in her front yard—a costly bit of landscaping that she was very happy with— Randi folded her arms and surveyed her property. Yep. She still felt certain the place spoke to her.

So why in hell didn't she feel complete?

She could get a pet. Except that she thought they were mostly nuisances.

Or a roommate. But yuck.

Maybe she needed surround sound. She was no electrician, but surely one of her brothers could be prevailed upon for their expertise. There had to be some benefit in putting up with four of them.

She couldn't ask Will—he was too busy being important as President of the university. And spending every spare minute of his life with his adorable baby girl.

Randi was spending a lot of spare minutes with the little miracle herself.

So maybe Paul could help her out. He'd wired his attic a few years ago. Surround sound might just be the ticket.

Except she didn't really need it. She was perfectly happy with her stereo system. She had digital cable television, too.

Her neighbor passed by, walking her dog. The little thing peed on the edge of Randi's fertilized grass.

Maybe she needed a fence.

Yeah.

Looking around the perimeter of her front yard, noticing how it ran right off to the sidewalk without a by-your-leave, she nodded. That was it. She'd always had this image when she was growing up of a home with a picket fence. Probably got it from watching too many reruns of the *Donna Reed Show* or *Leave It to Beaver*.

Heaving a sigh of relief, Randi slid off her boulder and went back inside. Thank goodness that was settled. She probably didn't have time during this break to install a fence, which was fine with her; she could go to Phoenix and play golf.

But come spring break, she'd get this project done.

All her life needed was a white picket fence.

SUPERROMANCE

You are now entering

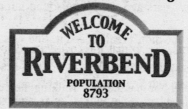

WELCOME TO **RIVERBEND**
POPULATION
8793

Riverbend...the kind of place where everyone knows
your name—and your business. Riverbend...home of
the River Rats—a group of small-town sons and
daughters who've been friends since high school.

The Rats are all grown up now. Living their lives and
learning that some days are good and some days
aren't—and that you can get through anything
as long as you have your friends.

Starting in July 2000, Harlequin Superromance brings
you Riverbend—six books about the River Rats and
the Midwest town they live in.

BIRTHRIGHT by **Judith Arnold** (July 2000)
THAT SUMMER THING by **Pamela Bauer** (August 2000)
HOMECOMING by **Laura Abbot** (September 2000)
LAST-MINUTE MARRIAGE by **Marisa Carroll** (October 2000)
A CHRISTMAS LEGACY by **Kathryn Shay** (November 2000)

Available wherever Harlequin books are sold.

HARLEQUIN®
Makes any time special ™

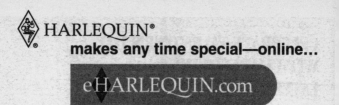

HARLEQUIN®

makes any time special—online...

eHARLEQUIN.com

shop eHarlequin

- ♥ Find all the new Harlequin releases at everyday great discounts.

- ♥ Try before you buy! Read an excerpt from the latest Harlequin novels.

- ♥ Write an online review and share your thoughts with others.

reading room

- ♥ Read our Internet exclusive daily and weekly online serials, or vote in our interactive novel.

- ♥ Talk to other readers about your favorite novels in our Reading Groups.

- ♥ Take our Choose-a-Book quiz to find the series that matches you!

authors' alcove

- ♥ Find out interesting tidbits and details about your favorite authors' lives, interests and writing habits.

- ♥ Ever dreamed of being an author? Enter our Writing Round Robin. The Winning Chapter will be published online! Or review our guidelines for submitting your novel.

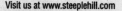